Heart
OF A
Jaguar

Marc Talbert

SIMON & SCHUSTER
BOOKS FOR YOUNG READERS

SIMON & SCHUSTER BOOKS FOR YOUNG READERS
An imprint of Simon & Schuster Children's Publishing Division
1230 Avenue of the Americas, New York, New York 10020
Copyright © 1995 by Marc Talbert
All rights reserved including the right of reproduction
in whole or in part in any form.
SIMON & SCHUSTER BOOKS FOR YOUNG READERS
is a trademark of Simon & Schuster.
Designed by Paul Zakris
The text of this book is set in 11-point Meridien.
Manufactured in the United States of America
10 9 8 7 6 5 4 3 2 1

LIBRARY OF CONGRESS CATALOGING-IN-PUBLICATION DATA
Talbert, Marc, 1953-
Heart of a jaguar / Marc Talbert.
p. cm.
Includes bibliographical references.
Summary: Balam, a Mayan boy struggling to achieve manhood, participates
in fasts, prayers, and rituals to appease the gods and bring rain to his village.
1. Mayas—Juvenile fiction. [1. Mayas—Fiction. 2. Indians of Mexico—
Fiction 3. Droughts—Fiction 4. Yucatán (Mexico ; State)—Fiction.] I. Title.
PZ7.T14145He   1995   [Fic]—dc20   94-41093
ISBN: 0-689-80282-X

For my daughters,
Molly and Jessie,
with love and hope

Acknowledgments

I am indebted to Charles Gallenkamp for his enthusiasm and his help in making this novel accurate. Any inaccuracies, however, are mine alone. Thanks also to the School of American Research library and to David Stuart for answering many questions with his wonderful answer to a single question asked over the phone. And loving thanks to my wife, Moo, who first introduced me to the Yucatán and was a wise and enthusiastic companion as I scrambled up temples and fought my way through bug-infested undergrowth in search of the spirit of the ancient Maya.

AUTHOR'S NOTE

Much of the Yucatán Peninsula, in the southern part of Mexico, is as flat as a tortilla. It is a land where the rivers run only underground, where nothing but the majestic temple ruins left by the ancient Maya interrupt vast stretches of the dense forest canopy. It is a land where the climate is often uncomfortably hot and humid, droughts occur with alarming frequency, and the soil is poor, but where one of the world's greatest civilizations flourished. This novel takes place around the year 1200 A.D., shortly after the collapse of the great Mayan city, Chichén Itzá, and several centuries before the arrival of the Spanish. I have not told a story of Mayan nobility, although the Maya in this story led lives as dignified and as exciting as the nobles portrayed in countless stone carvings found in the monumental buildings of *Chichén Itzá* and Uxmal. As honestly as I am able, I have told the story of Balam, a fourteen-year-old boy who lived in a village within a two-day walk from *Chichén Itzá*. We know relatively little about the peasant culture in which he lived—although there have been many exciting breakthroughs in our understanding within the past ten years. What we do know reveals a culture that was surprisingly advanced and profoundly beautiful, and very different from our own. I present this story of the Maya without apology and with reverence for their beliefs and practices. To make sense of the universe is not easy, even today with our modern technology and our cultural sophistication. Indeed, perhaps our technology and sophistication create barriers to making sense of the seen and unseen forces and things around us. We have much to learn from the Maya about the universe, and about ourselves.

Heart
OF A
Jaguar

Part I

Red from the East

Xkitzu ran into the *milpa*, calling her son's name with each breath. "Uk! Uk! *Uk!*" The maize plants, just taller than she was, shrugged their thin leafy shoulders and tossed their plumed heads, dancing, hunched, bending first one way and then the other.

As if one of the maize plants had come to life, Uk suddenly appeared, smiling. "Her time has come?" he asked. He would soon be a father and his mother would soon be a grandmother, a *chichi,* both for the first time. Pride deepened his smile.

"There is trouble!" Xkitzu gasped. She had run hard. Where her smock-like *huipil* clung to her, flesh colors showed through. A faintness floated over her. In that momentary darkness the maize looked more like shadowy men than before, the ears erect, brazen as naked men eager to make love.

Uk reached out and steadied her. "What is happening?" he asked, his smile wilting.

"Fetch Ah Chan! The midwife was called to Tzebtun and Ah Chan is the only one who will know what to do."

"Ah Chan?" Uk asked, as if he hadn't heard correctly.

"Yes," she swallowed. "Run!" She watched her son disappear into the forest. Closing her eyes she called to the goddess of the moon, of birth, the wife of Lord Sun, the mistress of Venus. "Ix Chel! Be with X'tactani. Help her now as she gives birth."

These words were followed by a groan. Xkitzu

opened her eyes and shook her head. This was the time of no moon. For a day and a night and a day no moon would appear in the sky.

Ix Chel could not help.

H   H   H

It was the fourteenth month, the month of Kankin, the Yellow Sun, and the morning was hot—perfect for growing maize. X'tactani had been hoping that the pains would ease a little, that the birth of her child would wait a few hours. It was an unlucky, even dangerous, day on which to give birth for both mother and child: the twelfth day of the month. It was also the day of Ben, the Reed, a weak day with no power to counteract bad luck brought by the number twelve. Ben, the twelfth of Kankin, was a forbidding combination.

She tried to calm the turmoil that stirred inside with the child. At the altar in her *palapa* she smeared a dab of ground maize mixed with honey on the mouth of the clay figure of Ix Chel. Surely so powerful a goddess would be able to help. To the child inside she chanted, "Wait, wait, little one. Wait, wait." The next day would be different. A child born on the thirteenth day of the month would most certainly have good luck in life. And even better, the next day was Ix, that of the Jaguar, the guardian of *milpa* and village both. It was a wonderful combination: Ix, the thirteenth, would bring much luck for a child born on that day.

But her water had broken just after her husband left

to work in the *milpa*. She had kept track of the pains, regular and growing closer together, wondering if there was anything she could do to slow them, to make them wait until Lord Sun was at his zenith, when the new day would begin. She tried to breathe slowly. She tried thinking of her husband's handsome face. Should she tell her mother-in-law, Xkitzu, what was happening? Should they send for the midwife? No. That would make giving birth certain to happen sooner rather than later. Instead she thought again of her husband's face, brushing the sweat from her own.

And then came a pain that clawed her insides. Blood followed, gushing as hot as the water earlier, only thick. She'd screamed to Xkitzu, who appeared at the doorway, her hands crusted with the meal of the soaked maize she was grinding.

The pain was so great she could force no words from her clenched mouth. She didn't need to. Xkitzu had seen the red blossoming on X'tactani's *huipil,* had seen the red streaming down her legs, puddling on the dirt floor. The old woman turned, calling from the *palapa* door for help from the family next door. And then she disappeared. Nakin, sweet, slow, bumbling Nakin, had come, and cradled X'tactani's head in her arms. A searing pain once more tore at her insides, feeling like the mauling claws of a jaguar. X'tactani fainted.

When she awoke, Ah Chan was standing over her, and a stink filled her nose. In haste he had brought her out of sleep with a crushed beetle. Its fumes made her eyes sting and her stomach writhe. She tried to push it away but couldn't. He cradled her in his arms now, bringing her upright and squatting, to help the child within drop from the yawn between her legs.

"There is no time for the drink that will ease your pain," he said. "When the pain comes again, push it out . . . with all your strength, push the pain out . . . and the child with it!" She detected fear in his voice, and sweat glistened on the great expanse of his brow. Behind Ah Chan, X'tactani saw her husband, Uk. Was it sweat or tears sliding down his face? She could not bear to see his face twisted so. Turning to Ah Chan she whispered, "What day is it?"

"Ben," Ah Chan whispered, placing his hand on her stomach. "The day of Ben." He caught his breath. "I feel the pain coming. Push . . . push!"

As if by his command, the pain came again and she shrieked, feeling blood run down the insides of her thighs, feeling as if her legs were being pulled in opposite directions—splitting her in two.

"A foot!" gasped Uk.

That was the last voice X'tactani heard.

H   H   H

Uk looked down at his wife. She lay in their bed, on her back, her belly shrunken now, looking unnaturally hollow. In death her face was growing relaxed—a peace-fulness had replaced the anguish and the pain. On her chest lay a baby boy, his purple face turned toward the nipple of his dead mother. He had come out backwards, twisted, and would never again move, or breathe or cry.

From behind came the cry of the baby boy who had surprised them all by following the first. It was the cry of a little voice, but in it could be heard all the pain of Xibalba—the Underworld—all the pain that now filled Uk. After the first baby had been pulled from its mother's body, the other baby had come, almost like an afterthought, swiftly and easily as afterbirth should have, but that never came.

Twins. Uk had fathered twins.

He looked at his hands. His fingers were crusted with drying blood. When the living boy came out, Ah Chan had put a reed knife in his hand. Uk had cut the cord between mother and son over several ears of maize held by Ah Chan. The blood had spurted once, catching Uk in the face, in the eyes, and then drained onto the maize.

It should have been a joyful act, the shedding of blood on maize—releasing from the blood its *ch'ulel,* the common soul of men and gods, the spirit of mother and child. It should have been a joyful act, letting the life in the blood soak into the maize, enriching the seeds for his son's first *milpa,* his son's blood crop. But he had done it clumsily, stupidly as a drunken monkey. Turning now, he walked from the *palapa,* into the courtyard. Tears came to his eyes and, to keep them from falling, he looked to the sky. Looking through the tears was like he imagined it would be looking up through the deep water of a *cenote*. A sensation of bobbing in such a sinkhole's water suddenly filled him with dizziness—bobbing with each breath, more down than up. And then, bubbling as if from a *cenote's* depths, from Xibalba itself, came a cry of rage, of disbelief.

Sorrow seemed to echo in the emptiness left by the sound. He felt a hand on his shoulder and from behind came the weary voice of his old friend, Ah Chan. "I was too busy to know if Lord Sun reached his zenith. I cannot be certain. But I think the second son was born on this day of Ix . . . on the thirteenth day of the month. If this is so, we must cling to the hope . . . to the hope that good fortune will follow the boy from this day forward."

For many days, whenever Uk looked at his son, he wondered: On what day, truly, was this boy born? What would the future hold for his boy? Would his future be one of luck? Or one of misfortune?

ONE

Balam let the other boys swarm ahead on the trail. They jumped and laughed as they ran over sunshine broken up by lengths of thin shadow, pretending the shadows were snakes crossing the trail. Some of the shadows slanted down from the tree branches, slithering over the bare bodies jumping through them. The mute dog who always followed his younger half-brother, Tooch, jumped and twisted, spooked by the way the boys were acting. But then it was spooked by most everything.

Tooch yelled over his shoulder, "Hurry, Balam, or the snakes will get you."

Balam continued to dawdle. "Jaguars aren't afraid of snakes," he called. He then bared his teeth and growled loudly, spreading his fingers as if they were claws raking the air. His name, Balam, meant "jaguar" and it was his favorite thing to pretend to be. In practiced mock horror, the boys yelled and spurted ahead. The dog tucked tail and tongue and streaked ahead of the children, looking back at Balam with big eyes, expressing real horror. If it could have made sounds it would have yelped.

Balam couldn't help smiling. Sometimes it was fun to be the oldest boy child in the village, to be considered the leader by the other boys. He kicked at a shadow, watching it cut across the top of his foot. They trusted him to know things, even when he didn't, and to be brave, even when he wasn't. When Balam settled a quarrel among them, his wisdom was seldom questioned.

But there were times, like now, when he grew bored of their games, jokes, and fights. Lately he felt more like a girl tending toddlers than like a leader of boys. It was becoming harder for Balam to imagine that shadows were snakes. It was becoming harder for him to be good-natured about wrestling all these boys at once, pretending to let them kill and flay him, the man-eating jaguar, and then to rise from the dead, angry and dangerous. It was becoming harder for him to take their little quarrels seriously enough to pass careful judgment.

At fourteen he was eager to cut off the white bead he had worn on a length of his hair since he was four years old. Every boy in the village had such a bead. To cut it off meant leaving childhood behind, meant standing in the doorway to adulthood, listening and observing even if he could not yet enter. To cut it off meant wearing an *ex* about his thickening boyhood. It would mean being able to live in the bachelor *palapa* at the edge of the village, where Tutz—the leader of boys before Balam—had gone to live almost two years ago. And not long after that it would mean clearing a *milpa* for his own blood crop . . . then a wife . . . and children.

But the bead still bounced against the back of his neck and the other village boys would not leave him alone. Each morning, they came to the courtyard of his family's *palapa*, pestering him to play, teasing and joking and whining until he gave in—or until his *chichi* threw him out with all the other boys.

Balam looked ahead and saw that the boys were standing in a clump, blocking the trail, waiting for him to draw near. What surprise were they planning? Balam decided to act first. He hunched his shoulders and lifted his lips into a snarl. Crouching, he made his eyes wild and roared.

Delighted, the boys squealed, spinning around and racing down the trail, eager to be chased. Balam took this opportunity to slip into the forest on his left. None of the boys saw him do this, but even if they had Balam knew none were brave enough without his own leadership to leave the trail and follow. He wondered, himself, if he should be walking alone in the forest, away from the trail. But at the moment, he preferred the possible danger of real snakes to pretending shadows were snakes.

Now that he was alone, where should he go? The dryness in his mouth answered for him.

It was not far to the *cenote*, the sinkhole where the village fetched its water. All his life he had been warned not to play near the *cenote's* edge. To fall into its waters meant certain death, more horrible still because Xibalba lurked just under the water's surface. The adults in the village should have known better: Such warnings made playing around the *cenote* irresistible to young boys— especially after fighting pretend jaguars and snakes in the heat of the day—and winning every battle.

As he picked his way through the forest, Balam listened for danger. Off to his right was a rustling that could have been made by an iguana but he couldn't be certain what it was. With no rain the leaves and twigs on the forest floor were more brittle than ever. An ant could sound almost like an iguana. An iguana could sound like a peccary and a jaguar, usually almost silent, might now sound like a deer.

He heard the noise again—closer this time. What could be making this noise? And was it dangerous? No, Balam told himself. The most dangerous animals, such as jaguars, were quieter than what he'd heard. He crouched behind a pumpwood bush, searching the undergrowth, hoping it was an iguana he could take to his *chichi* for eating. What a treat that would be! Since the drought, animals had grown scarce, died off or gone to wherever there was rain and water.

But just because animals were scarce did not mean the same was true of *yum kaax*, the forest spirits. Off from where the noise had come Balam saw a young ceiba tree. Could a *xtabai* have made those noises? His heart thumped at the thought. Sometimes, when they saw a man, those beautiful women spirits emerged from the trunks of the ceiba trees in which they lived. They would emerge with their arms open, their lips ready to be kissed, dressed in *huipils* of great beauty. But woe to the man who hugged a *xtabai*, who felt the thorny woodenness of her back! To hug or kiss a *xtabai*, to lust after one's hollow beauty, was to go mad.

Balam peered through the bush. He saw nothing. Was he man enough to draw the attention of such a spirit? Part of him hoped so—while another part of him was relieved to think a *xtabai* wouldn't bother with him, naked boy that he was.

Balam stood and continued toward the *cenote*. The sounds of birds told him he was drawing near.

At the *cenote* he dropped to his knees, grasping the edge with both hands. Because of the drought, his *chichi* had told him to check before drawing water. What animals remained in the forest sometimes became crazed with thirst, jumping into the water and fouling it, trapped by the *cenote's* sheer high walls, finally sinking, adding to the stink of Xibalba.

Balam looked beyond the ribs of rock curving away from him. Many hand spans below, at the *cenote's* heart, the water was calm and smooth. The *cenote* was round, the shape of an eye looking up, filled with water and sunken into the skeletal face of the earth. Only leaves floating here and there marred its smooth surface. The clear sky shone on the water, making it blue. A blue eye? Balam chuckled at such a ridiculous idea.

Leaning over as far as he dared, Balam looked down in fascination at the small face looking up at him.

"Hello," Balam whispered to the face. He smiled, and the boy in the water smiled back, showing how beautifully his front teeth were filed to points. Balam's smile collapsed. Had the face in the water smiled a moment too late? Was it his face, or the face of his twin who had died being born?

Balam stared at this face and it stared back. What would it have been like to grow up with a twin? Would he and his brother have looked alike and thought alike? Would they have acted alike? Would he and his twin have been as clever as the Hero Twins Ah Chan told stories about, tricking the gods of death in Xibalba? Or would his brother have been bad when he was good, noisy when he was quiet, frowning when he smiled?

As these questions tangled his thoughts, a breath of air ruffled the water's surface. The face below broke up, bending this way and that until, for a moment, he saw the larger face of a jaguar instead of a boy. It opened its mouth and flattened its ears. Balam gasped, feeling suddenly lightheaded, as if he were about to pitch forward. He grasped the edge of the *cenote*. Crumbs of dirt and limestone broke off, falling into the water, onto the jaguar's face. The water slowly calmed and the pieces of a boy's face—his own face?—came together, back to their proper places.

What had he just seen? Had he glimpsed his companion spirit, perhaps? He'd heard stories of *uays*—people who could turn themselves into animal forms. Who hadn't heard such stories? Had he turned into a jaguar as he looked down into the water? Perhaps the jaguar he'd seen had been a joke played on him by somebody from the Underworld. His long-dead brother, perhaps?

Trembling slightly, Balam pulled back from the *cenote's* edge and stood. Did he dare draw water from the spot where a jaguar's face had stared? What other tricks—less playful, more dangerous—could be played on him? Balam squared his shoulders, ashamed of such fears. I am almost a man, he told himself, reaching for the *cenote's* calabash, tied to a long rope of twisted guind tree bark that was itself tied to a nearby tree. He threw it out, over the *cenote*, letting the rope run through his hands. When the calabash hit water he tugged, helping water slop inside.

Brave as he wanted to be, he braced himself as the calabash filled. If he'd seen his brother's face in the water instead of his own, would his brother tug at the rope and pull him in? Did his brother want the company of a twin in that world the way he, Balam, sometimes wanted the company of a twin in this world?

Balam pulled up the calabash, hand over hand, feeling for tell-tale wiggles, for extra weight, wondering if he was pulling up more than water. As he dropped to one knee, reaching to ease the calabash over the *cenote's* edge, a hand grabbed his shoulder. Gasping, he pictured an *aluxob,* one of the forest elves who played pranks on careless people. As small as they were, *aluxob* were strong—sometimes deadly. Balam let go of the rope and hugged the ground, hoping he was too heavy for an elf to lift. A moment later the calabash splashed, hitting water. Balam did not want to follow it.

Familiar laughter bounced around the *cenote's* walls. Balam didn't need to look to know who had just played a trick on him.

The bachelor, Tutz, grinned as he helped Balam stand. Through the blackness painted on Tutz's chest were the welts of a new tattoo. Balam longed for one too. "Sorry, Balam. I didn't know it was you. I thought instead that I was catching the ugliest monkey of all stealing the *cenote's* calabash. But no monkey could be *that* ugly, I told myself. I saw no tail in the back!" Tutz laughed again, looking pointedly at Balam's nakedness. "But there it is . . . a tiny tail . . . in the front!"

Tutz should have known better. In all of the years they had played together as boys, he'd never been able to get the best of Balam's angry tongue.

"Is that why you now wear an *ex*?" Balam asked, each word pouncing, glaring at the loincloth wrapped around Tutz's waist and between his legs. "Do you wear an *ex* to hide the tail you have in back instead of in front?"

Tutz laughed once more, but there was no joy in it. His face began to harden. Balam immediately regretted what he'd said. He had indeed gotten the better of Tutz in the game of words, but his own temper had gotten the better of him. It was foolish to make enemies of a bachelor, especially since he hoped soon to live among the bachelors.

But it was more than that. Tutz was the brother of Ix Bacal, the girl who had been promised as Balam's wife. Shouldn't the brother of one's wife also be one's friend?

"I see your tongue flicks at words the way a frog flicks at flies," Tutz said quietly. He reached for a large, battered calabash he'd brought with him from the bachelor *palapa*, pulling it closer. "Perhaps you could pull up some water for me, brother . . . help fill this calabash."

Tutz was ordering him to draw water from the *cenote*? Balam's eyes grew narrow with anger. But he kept his mouth closed and his feet rooted. Tutz knew. He knew that Balam needed the older boy's friendship more than Tutz needed his. More than anything, Balam wanted to walk away, refusing to be ordered around by Tutz. But he also knew the wisdom of drawing water. Tutz had given him a way to apologize without admitting wrong.

Silently, Balam stared at Tutz's face, imagining it was that of a toad. It was not so hard to do. He smiled at this thought, knowing that Tutz would give a flattering meaning to the smile. He reached for the rope of the *cenote's* calabash.

"You should visit the bachelor *palapa* sometime," Tutz said, relief sounding in his voice as Balam lifted the calabash over the *cenote's* edge. Balam was surprised—Tutz hadn't wanted to fight with him, either! "It's been a long time since we spent time together."

Tutz took the full calabash from Balam and tried to smile. But Balam did not trust it—Tutz's smile was as friendly as a crack in a clay pot. "But when you come, leave the boys behind. We men have no use for the chatter of monkeys with tails in front instead of in back."

TWO

Balam looked about him as he walked along the path toward his village. He longed for *yax*—the dark blue-green of the forest leaves after the daily rains began. It had been almost two years since the rains had fallen, since the last *hahah,* and that color of new corn and jade was gone from the forest. But then *yax* was more than a color. It was a smell—of new leaves, moist soil, and flowers. It was a sound—of bird song and frog grunts, of bees humming and drops of water slipping from leaves. It was a feel—of soft air become playful, touching skin like a breath of laughter.

Now, all around, Balam could see nothing but the bone-like grays of wilted leaves, stained with patches and streaks of brown the color of dried blood. He smelled only rot, and only brittle sounds broke the silence. Already, even before Lord Sun was high enough to peer down through the trees, it was so hot birds—what birds there were—had stopped singing.

Even the sounds of the village were different after a year of drought. No longer did the village ring with the cries of penned turkeys—most had been eaten or offered as food to the gods of the thirteen heavens. And no dogs ran to greet him. Only three dogs were left in the entire village when once there had been nearly a full count—twenty. One was the castrated, barkless dog that followed Tooch about. Poor Tooch believed he was protecting this one. Unlike their cousins who barked, this kind of dog was raised for eating or sacrificing. Nobody spoke of it, but even barking dogs had been secretly, quietly eaten.

Before entering the village, Balam stopped at the carefully tended grove of breadnut trees. It was largely upon the fruit of these trees that the village had grudgingly lived in the absence of maize. Balam looked about for fallen breadnuts to take to his *chichi* or to his stepmother, Nakin. He saw only one that looked good. Even breadnuts were becoming scarce.

He walked through the village, to the square plaza at its center. With heat shimmering off its packed earth, the plaza looked very much like a watery place where the boundaries between Xibalba and this world were blurred. In the heart of the plaza grew a giant ceiba tree. Nobody in the village spoke of it, but the sacred tree was dying. As he walked by, Balam avoided looking at it. He did not want to see the patches of sky showing through branches that were almost bare of leaves. He did not want to see that what leaves remained were sickly, more gray than green.

What does it mean, Balam wondered, when a sacred ceiba tree dies? His godfather, Ah Chan, had told him often that the ceiba separated heaven and hell, held them apart yet connected them—held apart the four directions, yet connected them—helped those bearded giants, the *Bacabob*, hold up the sky at its four sides, allowing the middle world of rock and maize and people to exist. When a sacred ceiba tree dies, does everything it connects fly apart? Or does everything fall inward, crushing rock, maize, and people?

These questions made Balam uncomfortable. Ah Chan often told him that he had more questions than an opossum had fleas. It was with great relief that Balam saw the white-washed wall of loosely stacked stones surrounding the thatched *palapas* of his family's compound. Stepping through a gap in the wall, he entered the courtyard, determined to leave these questions behind.

He looked to his left, to the place where his mother was buried along with his twin brother. The packed dirt over them was smooth—a stranger would be unable to tell what was underneath. And now he, too, was uncertain. He had felt very strongly the presence of his twin at the *cenote*. Did his mother also stray from the place where she was buried?

Often, Balam greeted her when he entered the courtyard. He hoped that she knew him well, and loved him, having overheard him grow up, playing in the courtyard, sharing his troubles and adventures with her when nobody else would listen. It had been a while since he had greeted her, and he was about to walk over, squat next to her, tell her about his experience at the *cenote,* when his *chichi* rushed from the main *palapa,* a finger to her lips.

"You must be quiet!" she said, her voice rumbling even as a whisper. "Nakin is feeling unwell."

Balam nodded, silently handing the breadnut to his *chichi.* Instead of showing gratitude, disgust puckered her wrinkled face. Balam eyed the breadnut critically. It was not good enough?

"It was the only one on the ground. . . ." he began, angry that he felt obliged to apologize for a gift.

His grandmother's face relaxed. "No, no," she mumbled. She tried to speak quietly, but succeeded only in sounding more gruff. "I am not upset with you, Balam . . . or the breadnut. I am only angry that we have eaten nothing but breadnuts for many months. Breadnuts! They fill the stomach, but they do not nourish the heart, replenish *ch'ulel,* in the same way as maize." She raised the fruit to her face and hissed, "First Father made people from maize, not this."

She turned to go but, to Balam's astonishment, she spun all the way around, facing him again. It was the most graceful thing he'd ever seen his *chichi* do—almost as graceful as the twirl of a young girl. She too seemed astonished by what she'd just done, her mouth stretching into a rare, awkward smile.

"I almost forgot," she said. "Fetch Ah Chan for Nakin. She is asking for him." This time when she turned, her firm steps led to the door of the *palapa,* and then inside.

H   H   H

Most of the time Balam loved to visit Ah Chan, his godfather and the village *ahman,* the priest. The old man told wonderful stories—the making of the first people, the constant battles between the spirit world and men, of the Hero Twins and the struggles between the gods in the thirteen heavens and the seven Lords of Death in Xibalba. He spoke of these things with authority—in trances he could travel freely between Xibalba and the heavens and the middle world of men. And he was the only one in the village who talked often of life in Chichén Itzá before it was invaded. Sometimes he even spoke of how he'd helped a handful of men and women and children to flee Chichén Itzá—his mother and father among them. He had chosen this place to settle. The lone, ancient ceiba tree had told him that a Mayan village had once been here and that a forgotten *cenote* must be nearby.

But there were times when a look from Ah Chan could bruise like a stone. He was a tall man—of royal blood, from people who had eaten meat daily for generations—with a voice that could roar with the anger of a cornered jaguar. His moods could change quickly—anger striking like lightning from a clear sky, a caress coming from a hand poised to slap. If anyone could be an *uay* in this village—could change themselves into an animal of any kind—it was Ah Chan.

Balam approached the old man's *palapa* cautiously. Most people did these days. For the past year Ah Chan's moods had grown as dark as rain clouds that he prayed would come, but didn't.

Ah Chan was sitting in the shade of his doorway, staring toward the village ceiba tree. He sat, looking almost drained of life, of *ch'ulel*, a frown further withering his face. Quietly, Balam approached, lowering himself onto his haunches. Was Ah Chan traveling, visiting Xibalba or conversing with Itzamná, the most powerful lord of the heavens?

Balam grew uncomfortable staring at the old man. He turned his gaze to the tree. Its canopy seemed to have shrunk, causing its bulky, enormous trunk to look as bloated as something dead. Could it be dying from some poison rising from Xibalba, coming up through roots that spread as far and deep as the branches reached upward and out? If that were possible, what could stop those in Xibalba from sending poison upward through the roots of maize or breadnut trees? Or upward through the water of a *cenote*?

Balam was startled by Ah Chan's voice. "Perhaps it is time for this tree to die," he said, as if he were answering the questions in Balam's mind. He often surprised

Balam by seeming to know what he was thinking. Balam looked at him and was relieved to see Ah Chan's face returned to life.

"But if the rains come . . ."

"Perhaps then it will live." Ah Chan often interrupted Balam's questions.

"If it dies will we plant another?" Balam asked.

"If it dies, the village will die also," Ah Chan said without emotion. Balam had heard him say this before, but hoped he'd changed his mind since. He turned now to look at Balam. "What brings you here?"

"Nakin," Balam said. "My stepmother is not feeling well and is asking for you."

The old man grunted as he stood. Stooping, he walked into his *palapa* and returned a moment later carrying a pouch in which he kept incense, roots, and leaves to help with sickness. Balam had helped him find much of what was in the pouch. What Ah Chan didn't have in the pouch could easily be found in the forest. Sometimes only words or song were needed, or a correct touch.

They walked silently to Balam's *palapa*. Striding behind Ah Chan through the gap in the stone wall made the courtyard feel smaller, less important. It took only a few of Ah Chan's steps to Balam's several to reach the main *palapa* at the head of the courtyard. Balam followed him inside, into dim coolness.

Chichi looked up from where she knelt by Nakin's bed. With the good manners she reserved for all men, she averted her eyes and face from Ah Chan and drew back a respectful distance. Balam wished she showed him such respect, but also found himself wanting to know what she was thinking and feeling behind the blank face she now wore in Ah Chan's presence.

Nakin lay on her side, curled up, her back to them. The old man rested an open hand on the round of her hip.

"Please, *Chichi*, I wish to sleep," Nakin muttered, trying to push the hand away.

"I am here," Ah Chan said, quietly.

Startled, Nakin sat up, her eyes wide, looking at Ah Chan before modestly bowing her head.

Ah Chan gazed down at her, his hand now resting on Nakin's head. Balam saw Nakin's shoulders trembling. Was her illness that serious, that painful?

As he watched, the love he felt for Nakin ran through him, strong as blood. It was a love wanting to protect her from the embarrassment of mistaking Ah Chan for his *chichi*—a love wanting to make her well again and happy. His love for Nakin had been nourished well, growing as he grew, having begun with suckling her after his mother died. She was the only mother he'd ever known. It was true she was often slow and bumbling. He had even heard some people whisper that his father married Nakin because he could not bear to marry a pretty or smart woman, that he could never marry somebody who would remind him of X'tactani, the woman who had given Balam birth.

But Nakin was as kind and gentle as she was slow and bumbling. How could Balam not love her? Nobody laughed harder at her own mistakes than she did. Nobody encouraged Balam more when he did poorly, or praised him more when he did well.

Ah Chan felt Nakin's pulse, listening to her blood, first at her wrist and then at her elbow. Taking a step away from her, his hand fell to his own side. "What is it you wish from me?" he asked, his voice surprisingly gentle. "In thirteen months . . . two-hundred sixty days, more or less . . . you will return to normal. There is nothing wrong with you that giving birth will not cure."

Balam's eyebrows fluttered. Nakin with child? His heart rejoiced. He would count with his fingers and toes each day of each month. This child would come at the right time. When he, Balam, left to live in the bachelor *palapa,* Tooch would have somebody to look after, somebody to pester him as much as he'd pestered Balam all these years . . . even if the child was a girl. Especially if the child was a girl!

Nakin lifted her head, tears running down her face. "I was afraid this was so. Last night I dreamt of snakes." Her mouth trembled. "Why?" she asked, looking from Ah Chan to Balam and then to *Chichi.* "I fear for this child to come. I do not want to lose it to death, but I fear it comes at a bad time." She looked at Ah Chan, her eyes pleading. "One year of drought can be followed by another year of drought. With drought comes famine and with famine comes war. This is not a good time to have a child!"

Ah Chan let the silence linger after Nakin's words. When he spoke, his words seemed weary. "The gods are weak and we must do all we can to feed them before we become so weak our blood will not nourish them. Yes. We must feed them, just as they feed us. And when we have given them all we can give . . . when we have given them the best we can give . . . we must then accept what is to come."

"You read the stars. You read the divining stones. You once read what was written in the books at Chichén Itzá. What will come? Tell me what will come for my child!" Nakin spoke with an anger that chased her fear.

"I do not know. I wish I did, but I do not." The old man turned to *Chichi.* "Where is Uk?"

"This morning, when he heard of Nakin's dream, he went hunting. He believes Nakin will feel better with meat or wild honey . . . that those things will strengthen her . . . to avoid. . . ."

His *chichi* didn't need to finish her thought. Three times since Tooch was born, and once before, Nakin had endured losing a baby before it was meant to be born. Each time she grieved more than the last. Each time Uk could have left her for another wife. He hadn't and nobody thought he ever would.

"When he returns, send him to me. We must talk."

With that, the old man turned and brushed past Balam. The door seemed to blink and he was gone.

THREE

Balam rose from his bed, hoping he'd awakened early enough to hunt with his father. The only other person in Nakin's bed was Tooch, sprawled over most of it.

"*Wac!*" he cursed, listening to the thump-thump outside of his *chichi* grinding breadnuts into paste for making tortillas. He walked out of the *palapa* and around to the cooking shed, trying to frustrate his disappointment with the hope that his father might still be eating breakfast. If so, he could still join in hunting.

What he saw surprised him more than if his father had been there. Ix Bacal was grinding chunks of breadnut, not his *chichi*, who was flipping tortillas back and forth on the hot slab of rock—the *opps*—that straddled the three stones of her cooking fire. As the young girl bent over the *metate*, Balam was amazed to see she now had small breasts—small but large enough to jiggle lightly as she pounded rock against rock.

She is growing, he thought, becoming a woman. And because they were almost the same age, Balam was especially pleased to think that, likewise, he must be growing into manhood.

Lately he'd tried to speak first in the morning, as a man should. But this morning his *chichi's* voice startled him from his staring. "You are late this morning. Again." He turned to her. In the sleepy light of dawn her wrinkled face reminded him of an overripe papaya.

"My father has left?"

"Of course," his *chichi* growled.

Balam retreated from his *chichi's* vexed eyes by looking at Ix Bacal. He was relieved to see that Ix Bacal continued to work as if he was not there, averting her gaze, treating him as a woman should treat a man. Was he, her future husband, a man in her eyes? Or was she just extending to him the politeness of silence, allowing him to hope that she was too involved in her work to hear the way his *chichi* treated him like a boy? Either way, he preferred her manners—as well as her looks—to those of his grandmother.

As he enjoyed her beauty, his heart seemed to beat in rhythm to her pounding—thump! thump! thump!—and the echoing bounce of her breasts. To still the fluttering in his chest and stomach, Balam looked at his grandmother. Her interest now was directed at the tortillas steaming on her *opps*. She stared at them the way she'd stared at him.

Lately she was always grumpy. Why? Do people turn sour, like overripe fruit, when they grow old? Was there anything he could do to make her happy, to make her smile? Surely such a feat would not go unnoticed by Ix Bacal.

"May I fetch water for you, *Chichi*?" he asked.

He was relieved to see her face soften as she handed him several tortillas that were almost too hot to handle. "Go! Go on!" She shooed him with a wave of her hand. "Ix Bacal is here to help while Nakin is not well. If you want to help, fetch firewood. We are nearly out."

"Yes, *Chichi*," he said. He stole a glance at Ix Bacal and caught her glancing at him. The twinkle in her eyes told him she was amused by what she'd witnessed. He smiled quickly, hoping she saw his beautifully filed teeth before once more bowing her head over the grinding stone.

As he walked and chewed, joy shone brightly in Balam, seeming to match the growing strength of the sun. He did not wish Nakin ill, but perhaps now he would see more of Ix Bacal in the days to come.

Without the clatter of Tooch and the other boys, he could hear clearly the forest sounds—the birds and an occasional, distant call of monkeys. Gentle puffs of air set the drying forest leaves to rattling, reminding Balam of the sound of rain, which he hadn't heard for a very long time. Tooch and the boys could never be quiet enough. Wherever they went, their noise warned creatures all around to fly or slither or skitter away.

As he finished the last tortilla, Balam silently renewed his promise to fetch wood for the cooking fire. But first he wanted to take advantage of being alone to do a little hunting. He didn't have a knife or a spear—he would only be able to hunt animals small enough to hit with a rock or stick or to catch with his hands. If he caught something his *chichi* would have to be impressed. Even if she wasn't, catching something would undoubtedly impress Ix Bacal.

Balam made his way to where he'd heard the rustling noise in the forest yesterday, on his way to the *cenote*. With animals so scarce that his father came back empty-handed more often than not, Balam thought it was a likely place to start.

As he walked, he sent out a silent prayer to Ah Ceh, the god of the chase, of hunting, asking for success. Did Ah Ceh listen to boys, or only to men? Regardless, Balam promised he would save part of whatever he caught as an offering, as food, for Ah Ceh.

The closer he got, the slower and quieter he walked. Even though he would only be able to catch something small, he listened for deer. If he heard or saw one, his father could search for it later. Looking for deer was tricky, though—if he saw one, his father might not believe him. Deer were protected by *zip*, crafty forest creatures who often transformed themselves into small deer, leading hunters away from real deer. *Zip* could also make iguanas look like deer. Balam had known many a hunter to come back with an iguana, only to claim that he was certain he'd felled a deer instead.

Balam heard his father's voice in his head: *To catch something, first decide what it is you want to catch and then picture it in your mind.* Balam tried to remember clearly the noise he'd heard. At the time, he'd thought it was made by an iguana. Perhaps, though, it had been made by an armadillo. But if I picture an armadillo, Balam reasoned, and it is an iguana, I will be unprepared for the iguana's speed. On the other hand, if I picture an iguana and it is an armadillo, I'll move so fast I'll catch the armadillo before it can curl into a ball.

He pictured an iguana—crest up, tongue darting, its green head lifted and still, eyes alert.

But there was more to hunting than picturing the prey. One must also think like the animal one wanted to kill. Where would an iguana go to escape a clever hunter?

As if in answer to this question, Balam heard scurrying to his right and, from the corner of his eye, saw the flick of a tail. Had he seen a snake or an iguana? He pictured an iguana so clearly that even if it were a snake it might be turned into an iguana by the power of what he pictured. It must be an iguana, he decided. Snakes made softer noises, even now with dry leaves piled so deep. And snakes don't dart this way and that. They slip across the ground, moving like a stream of spilled water, thinning as it disappeared into the earth.

He bent over, far enough so his hands could touch the ground, to push him off to the right or the left while his legs sent him forward, and also to keep him from falling onto his face while letting him grab what he was chasing. Ahead was a low pile of tumbled limestone blocks, the rubble of an old Maya building. He paused for a moment. In ruins there lived spirits, not all of them good. But it was now daytime. And these blocks of stone made the kind of place iguanas liked to hide.

Think like an iguana! he told himself. He crept to the rocks, trying to move like an iguana, his tongue tempted to dart in and out, his eyes jumping this way and that as he looked for movement. He squatted in the shade of a coral bean bush, watching for motion just as an iguana might—his head raised, his arms planted apart, elbows bent outward, tensed and ready.

For a moment he wondered if it were possible to think so much like an iguana he might turn into one.

He didn't have time to ponder this. To his left, where he least expected, an iguana's head popped up from behind a rock and stared at him. Balam caught his breath and prepared to jump. The head disappeared.

Balam crept to his right, keeping the rock on his left within sight. Suddenly a head popped up in front of him. The same iguana? Balam prepared to pounce but the iguana disappeared.

He was pleased that he'd been thinking enough like an iguana to anticipate where it would pop up. But as much as he tried to think only like an iguana he was also thinking like himself. As he squatted and waited, his thoughts grew confused. It seemed the iguana in his head, the one he was trying to think like, now knew what he was thinking. He moved a little to his right just as he saw an iguana's head to his left. As he moved to his left, the head disappeared. It seemed that both the iguana and he knew what the other thought, and were going around in circles both in his head and on the rocks.

Quietly, Balam picked up a stone that fit perfectly into the cup of his palm and fingers. His gut told him the iguana was straight ahead. His head told him it remained to his left. He went with his gut—cocking his arm and holding it in readiness.

Just as the iguana peeked over the rock ahead, Balam hurtled the stone. Balam heard a thud and scrambled up, reaching behind the rock. He felt the cool smoothness of iguana skin.

Quickly, he pulled it over the rock by a front leg and, as it dangled, grabbed the root of its tail with the other hand, letting go of the leg. He was pleased to see that the iguana was stunned, but not dead. To have killed it would cause its meat to spoil quickly in the heat of the day. Its mouth opened and its tongue flicked as it sprang to life, pawing the air and hissing.

Struggling to hold the iguana at arm's length, he scrambled down the rocks, sliding where dried, brittle moss crumbled under his hands and feet. His *chichi* would be pleased—it had hung to his waist.

Once off the rocks, Balam flipped the iguana onto the ground, stunning it again. Before it could once more spring to life, he stepped on its back, just above its hind legs, and bounced lightly. He heard a snap on the first bounce, telling him that he'd broken its back, paralyzing its hind legs and tail. Looking about, he pulled a length of stout grass and looped one end of it over the lizard's mouth. He wound the other end around each of its front legs, tying them together.

Balam was pleased. It wasn't fat, but it was plenty large. The iguana's eyes now followed him as he gathered wood, but it could not move. It would stay alive for a day or two, until his *chichi* decided to cook it.

Balam soon had enough wood for a good-sized bundle. Not many months ago, firewood had been scarce this close to the village. But as the dryness continued, trees were beginning to shed whole branches, almost as they shed leaves. Some trees had died altogether. It was at once a curse and a blessing not to have to search far for wood.

As he tied the bundle with a ribbon of bark, Balam looked to the sky. More time had passed than he thought. Lord Sun had already climbed past the crest of his path—a new day had begun. What day was it now? Balam wondered, balancing the wood on his shoulder with one hand, lifting the iguana by its tail with his other. Was it a lucky or unlucky day? Ah Chan would know. But right now, to Balam, with an iguana in his hand—feeling heavier in limpness—the day seemed very lucky indeed.

Balam hurried in spite of his awkward burden. He wanted to see his *chichi* try hiding her smile when she saw what he brought. Even more, he wanted Ix Bacal to see. And Tooch—wouldn't he be jealous! Balam kept his head down, concentrating on his footing, even as he joined the trail leading to the village.

⊣ ⊣ ⊣

Although Ix Bacal was gone when Balam arrived, his disappointment did not last long. When Nakin saw the iguana, she smiled for the first time in days, and clapped.

"Look at what you've brought us!" she said, as proudly as if she'd caught it herself.

"Don't tell us that you were certain it was a deer," said his *chichi*.

"But it was." Balam laughed. "It was a deer that I walked up to, charming it by singing softly. And then I jumped on its back, riding it like a jaguar, holding on with my hands and feet and teeth, wishing I had claws. Only when it died of fear and weariness, only then did I find myself on top of this iguana!"

How Balam wished Ix Bacal could have seen his *chichi's* grin. How he wished she could have heard Nakin's laughter.

Even Tooch, who was trying hard to act unimpressed, couldn't help laughing.

"You're growing into quite a man," said Nakin, her smile large.

Yes, thought Balam proudly, I am.

When his father came home, once more empty-handed, Balam was surprised to feel no disappointment. Instead he felt pride in knowing he'd caught something when his father had not. It was a strange, new feeling, one he didn't know if he liked.

"I am pleased," Uk said, looking at the iguana stretched out in the cooking shed. The animal watched *Chichi's* every move with baleful eyes, as if knowing that of all the people about she was the one who would kill it.

"I only did as you taught me," Balam said, trying to sound modest. "I pictured what I wanted to catch. I thought like an iguana."

"Keep strutting like that," his *chichi* said, "and you will turn into a turkey. Then we would eat well! A boy turkey to go with the corn we don't have!"

Hearing everybody's laughter, Balam realized how long it had been since he'd last heard such pleasant sounds.

"Go! Go! You stink worse than the things you hunt." *Chichi* shooed Balam and Uk from the kitchen. "Go wash yourselves."

Balam helped his father, filling the bowl for him and carrying it to the place they washed beyond the cooking shed. He held the bowl over his squatting father and poured water over his father's shoulders and back as his father rubbed himself, at the same time spreading water from his shoulders onto his chest and thighs. Tipping his head back, closing his eyes, he let Balam pour the last of the water onto his face.

Uk sputtered as water ran over his mouth. Tipping his head forward and opening his eyes, he sighed. "For a moment I felt as if I'd lifted my face to the rain." He shook his head, grinning as water rained onto Balam. "I would help you but I hear Ah Chan's voice approaching."

Balam listened, hearing it too. He nodded, smiling. Perhaps this too was a good sign.

Fetching water, he walked back to the washing spot, wondering why Ah Chan had come. Squatting, he leaned forward as he began to lift when he noticed something move inside the bowl.

Balam was stunned by what he saw. In the bowl was a small fish, as long as one of his fingers. The fish was almost transparent, having no color. Balam gasped. It had no eyes!

Ah Chan had spoken once of such a fish. Such fish, the old man had said, came from Xibalba, from caves below the *cenotes*. Such fish were blinded when they looked upon the unspeakable creatures who lived in the Underworld. But in Xibalba their blindness was a blessing.

Had Ix Bacal drawn this fish while fetching water? Who could have played such a trick on her? Balam thought of the face he'd seen reflected on the water and the way it had changed to that of a jaguar. What evil power did this fish hold?

As if the bowl had suddenly become hot enough to burn his fingers, it slipped to the ground. Water splashed onto his feet and legs, but the fish remained in the bowl, flipping this way and that. Leaping up, he ran toward the cooking shed.

"Father! Father!" He gasped.

Nakin looked up, startled, concerned. "Your father is with Ah Chan, consulting with one of the neighbors," she said. "It may be time to prepare for planting maize."

Spinning around, Balam ran, first to one neighbor and then another. To which neighbor had his father gone? When he finally found him, Balam was so out of breath he couldn't speak.

"What is it?" Uk asked, taking Balam by the shoulders, looking him in the face.

"I . . . I . . ." Balam struggled to speak, but couldn't.

"Is it Nakin?"

Once more Balam tried to speak, his face growing red with effort. But no words came. Assuming the worst, Uk let Balam go and turned.

Balam leapt, grabbing his father's hand. Stumbling and pulling, he led his father around the back of their *palapa*, to the bowl.

He stared, once more unbelieving. A line of large ants marched from the forest, into the bowl, and out again, back into the forest. They were the same kind of ants that cleaned the village of feces and rotted food and scorpions. Where the fish had been, there was nothing.

Had he imagined the fish? Had it really been there?

"What was it that brought the ants to the bowl?" Uk asked.

"A fish," Balam managed to gasp.

"A fish?" His father frowned.

"A fish . . . with no . . . no eyes!" He picked up a stick, ready to strike at the ants for taking the fish, for making a fool of him, but mostly to release the great fear he held inside from seeing the fish.

A weary voice came from behind. "Let the ants be," Ah Chan said. "They are only doing their proper work."

FOUR

The day that had seemed lucky with an iguana in his hand had shown its true nature. He watched the ants as their numbers dwindled and the line slowly disappeared. Before long it looked as if nothing had ever been in the bowl.

How had the ants known so quickly to come for the fish? Fish were rare in the village. Balam had heard of places where water gathered together in streams, slithering over the ground like giant snakes. He'd been told fish lived in such rivers, but there were no rivers near the village—and no fish. Perhaps its unique, exotic smell had caught the ants' attention.

When Ah Chan and Uk began to speak quietly, Balam was pleased they didn't ask him to leave. Was he almost a man in their eyes?

"What could this mean?" Uk asked.

"I don't know," replied Ah Chan. He turned to Balam. "Who fetched this water?"

"Ix Bacal."

Ah Chan returned his gaze to the bowl. When he finally spoke, he first stood, grunting. "I will go speak with her."

н н н

Where there had been laughter, now there was only silence. Nakin had been horrified upon learning of the fish. She had ordered Uk to take the calabash into the forest and bury it—and then retreated to her bed. His *chichi* had communicated anger less with her tongue, but more with her eyes, her walk, her heavy breathing.

Tooch had run off to tell his friends, and anyone else who would listen.

To escape the anger of his *chichi* and the fear of Nakin, Balam retreated to the courtyard, squatting next to the grave of his mother and brother. Was his mother aware of the strange things that had been happening to him lately? Was there something she wanted to tell him now, but couldn't?

These questions were interrupted by his father, who walked into the courtyard. He paused, contemplating his son. For the first time, Balam wondered if his father ever spoke to his first wife. Did he ever think of her buried in the courtyard? If so, Balam had never noticed. And now he was too uneasy to ask.

Instead, Balam stood.

"I am going to help Ah Chan purify the *cenote*," his father said. "It is a job only for a priest and his four helpers, and a few men."

He was about to protest, but his father turned and walked away. One moment Balam felt himself treated like a man and the next he was treated like a boy! Balam squatted again, dark thoughts filling his head like shadows during that murky time between night and dawn—when it is neither light nor dark—when it is difficult to distinguish between sky and earth, shadow and substance, the present and the past, between this world and the Underworld.

He stared at where his mother was buried, feeling caught, trapped, weighted down with anger the way she must be weighted down with dirt. Scrambling to his feet, he rushed from the courtyard, breaking into a run as he turned toward the bachelor *palapa*.

H   H   H

The bachelor *palapa* was part of the village, but set apart from it. Along the little-used trail Balam traveled, it was partly hidden from view by a clump of pumpwood bushes.

As he came within sight of the *palapa*, Balam grew shy. Tutz had invited him, but he wondered if he would be welcomed by the others. It was also possible Tutz had not been sincere in his invitation. Balam stepped off the path, hiding behind the large leaves of a guava bush. The clearing was quiet. Birds had stopped singing in the heat of the day. The bachelors were most likely inside napping—it was that time of day.

The *palapa* itself was not unusual—one room with a door facing east. What made it look different from other *palapas* was the way in which it was continually falling apart. Its thatched roof looked as if birds nested in it. The walls had occasional gaps in them where upright poles had fallen away. Instead of reattaching them, the bachelors sometimes shaped these poles into chopping sticks or clubs for hunting.

It looked much the same as when Balam first saw it, many years ago. When he was younger than Tooch, he and Tutz had made a game of spying on the bachelors.

Once, as they'd crawled through undergrowth, they'd heard yelling, cries of pain, and grunts. As they'd come to within sight of the *palapa,* Balam and Tutz had hidden as usual behind this very guava bush. From where he now stood, he'd seen several bachelors watching two other bachelors wrestling each other, and not in a friendly way—hitting and scratching and jabbing with elbows. These two bachelors were coated with dirt and some of the dirt was thickened with blood. Balam was amazed. He'd seen fights before in the village, but they'd always been between men who had drunk too much *balche* at celebrations. During that kind of fighting, the men were usually too drunk to do more than bloody each other's noses—or bloody their own noses from falling on their own faces.

But these bachelors were not drunk. They were quick and precise and strong enough to hurt each other badly. At every opportunity, one of them would grab at the other's *ex*, tearing and kicking. Finally, one of the bachelors ripped the *ex* off the other and, grabbing the other's testicles, paralyzed him with pain.

"She is mine?" he demanded. The other, who showed whiteness even through the dirt smeared over his body, nodded and then crumpled to the ground, moaning as he doubled up, cupping his crotch, vomiting in the dirt.

It was then Balam had noticed the woman. He'd never seen her before—she must have been from another village. She stood in a shadow in front of the *palapa*, her face blank and unsmiling. The victorious bachelor walked to her, taking her firmly by the arm, directing her into the *palapa*. She didn't seem eager to go with him, but she didn't resist.

It had seemed odd, what he had seen. And later, when he asked his father about it, he had told him that she was most likely a slave, a prostitute, brought from some village or other by the bachelors for a couple of days for several measures of maize. His father had told him they were most likely fighting over who would copulate with her first.

"Be careful in your spying," Uk had said. "An angry bachelor can be worse than a wounded peccary."

In spite of his father's warning, Balam and Tutz continued their spying. The bachelors, beyond the hearing and sight of their families, told lewd jokes and made whatever fun they wanted. Around their own *palapa,* the bachelors were not shy about being rude or cruel or ribald, loudly so. Twice more Balam had seen a prostitute there—once since Tutz went there to live.

These thoughts made Balam suddenly shy. He was not yet a bachelor. They would not be shy about making fun of him for being a boy, for wearing a bead in his hair and not wearing an *ex* or painting his body black.

Just as he was about to turn and sneak back to the village, Balam saw a bachelor emerge from the *palapa.* It was Keh, who was not the oldest bachelor but who was the leader among them. Whenever he was around Keh, Balam felt uneasy, as if Keh were looking for something to criticize, to make fun of. He watched as Keh disappeared around the back of the *palapa.*

Once more Balam was about to turn back to the village when Cantul walked from the *palapa.* He was the oldest of the bachelors—well-muscled, but not especially smart. Cantul should have been the leader of the bachelors, but he had deferred so often to Keh that nobody asked him questions anymore or expected him to make decisions. He seemed relieved by this arrangement, certainly not at all displeased, looking less worried now than when people had expected decisions or advice from him.

Cantul stood in the courtyard, as usual looking as if he were unsure why he was there, or even where he was. It was funny—enough so that Balam had to pinch the inside of his thigh to keep from laughing.

To Balam's relief, next out of the *palapa* was Tutz. He yawned and stretched, reaching for the sky as he walked.

Seeing Tutz gave Balam confidence about visiting the bachelors. To catch Tutz's attention, Balam made a call like a peccary, grunting three times from the back of his mouth, behind his tongue. When they had played together as boys it was their special call, to signal each other when they were pretending to hunt—or spying on the bachelors.

Tutz's eyes opened wide and his head turned toward where Balam crouched. Balam grunted three times more as Tutz lowered his arms and began to walk cautiously toward him. When he came to within a couple steps of the bush, Balam poked out his head and smiled.

Tutz stared a moment. A smile crept over his face.

"We used to hide behind that bush . . . you and I . . . and spy on the bachelors, didn't we?" he asked Balam.

Balam nodded. "But . . . but this time I wasn't spying. I came to visit."

"Visitors don't usually hide behind guava bushes," said Tutz. "Or grunt like peccaries."

While they were talking, neither Tutz nor Balam noticed Keh approaching until the older bachelor spoke.

"What are you hiding from us in the forest, Tutz?" he asked, a swagger in his voice that matched the swagger in his steps. "Did I hear a peccary? Or are you hiding from us a woman who will cook for you and clean for you and do your bidding?" He spoke loudly enough for the other bachelors to hear. Cantul approached, as usual looking befuddled. Several other bachelors came from the *palapa*, eager to take part in whatever mischief Keh had in mind.

Balam stepped from the bush, his ears burning. He struggled to control his anger, to control his tongue. He did not want to cause trouble among the bachelors, for himself or for Tutz. Soon he would live here. What could he say that showed boldness without being insulting? Before he could think of anything, Keh continued.

"But, Tutz, look at your woman. She is certainly ugly enough to scare away a peccary. Couldn't you have done better?"

Cuc, one of the approaching bachelors, laughed. "Keh, why are you so critical? I think she would be more than beautiful enough for you . . . if she would even have you." He glanced toward Balam, smiling, his eyes mischievous. "Your beauty, what little there is, would be wasted on Keh anyway."

Balam was unable to control his anger any longer. He stepped up to Keh and Cuc. Cuc feigned fright, stepping behind Keh, crouching in the shadow they both cast. "She grows more beautiful in anger," he said, and then hid his face.

Balam took one more step toward Keh, who tensed, ready to fight the boy. "Who sees a woman's beauty in the body of a boy? Have you been among men too long?" Balam shouted. Cuc stepped out from behind Keh, his mouth open in surprise. Anger replaced the mischief in his eyes.

There was a moment of stunned silence. Balam immediately regretted what he'd said. Would he ever be welcomed here after insulting the leader of the bachelors? And then, to Balam's surprise, Keh began to laugh.

"Your tongue is as sharp as the thorns of the subin tree." He turned to Tutz. "Who is your friend?"

"Balam," Tutz replied, sounding as relieved as Balam felt.

Keh's eyebrows arched. "The Balam who found a blind fish in his family's water calabash?"

Balam nodded, wondering how Keh knew. News of the fish must have traveled on the legs of ants, or on the lips of a half-brother with a big mouth.

"Come," Keh said, putting his arm around Balam in a friendly way. "Come tell us how it happened, with the fish."

All the bachelors gathered around, squatting in a circle. It was as if they all had a regular place to squat when they gathered in the courtyard.

For a moment Balam felt shy. All eyes were on him, every head tipped with interest.

"Tell us how it happened," Keh encouraged. And Balam did, haltingly at first and then with more confidence.

"Did you taste the water during the day . . . before

finding the fish?" asked a bachelor Balam didn't know well.

Balam shook his head. "No."

Cuc leaned forward. "I think the water from the *cenote* has been tasting odd lately." There was a murmur of agreement from around the circle.

"Yes," Keh said, a chuckle in his voice. "Especially when Cantul fetches it."

Tutz laughed. "Yes, when Cantul fetches the water he moves so slowly. . . ."

Balam struggled to look at each person who spoke—he found it difficult to move his eyes fast enough. "Very slow, even though I've never seen Cantul, lazy man that he is, fill the calabash more than half way. Still he moves so slow. . . ."

"So slow," interrupted another bachelor, "it tempts the monkeys in the trees. . . ."

"Yes! I've seen monkeys make sport of aiming down . . . at the calabash he carries," said another bachelor.

And yet another voice—Tutz's? "That's why his calabash is always full by the time he gets here."

"Full of yellow water!"

All the bachelors, including Cantul, began laughing too hard to continue with this story.

When the laughing stopped, Cuc spoke again, his voice and face serious. "I think the taste of the water changes when the level of the water in the *cenote* goes down, as it has."

Once more the bachelors murmured their agreement.

"What does Ah Chan think of the fish?"

Balam studied Keh's face, sensing anger in his question. Answering carefully, he said, "Ah Chan was troubled."

"He said no more?"

"No." What more should Ah Chan have said? Balam wanted to ask, but didn't.

"It is just as well," Keh continued. "We don't need Ah Chan to tell us the gods in heaven are weak, that the world is in chaos. He lives so much in the past . . . with his royal airs. I wonder if he even knows how serious our plight is."

Balam was surprised to hear a murmur of agreement from around the circle.

"He is nothing but a tired old man," Keh declared. "Lately nothing is going right and he has not been able to help us . . . or to help the gods. Perhaps he is losing his ability to speak with the gods, to travel to the Underworld or to heaven. And yet he refuses to train someone to take his place. We have heard he waits for you, Balam, to grow old enough to train."

Balam tried not to smile with pride. It was true Ah Chan took only him to gather incense, roots, and leaves to help with sickness and prayers. It was true that when Ah Chan told many stories—especially those of the Hero Twins—he looked only at Balam, as if expecting Balam to remember them and understand their importance.

Keh continued, scowling at Balam's smile. "We have

heard that until you come to live with us, our training in the ways of manhood will not resume. Perhaps . . ."

Cuc interrupted. "Perhaps Balam has heard enough." He turned to Balam. "We know Ah Chan is your godfather and that he and your father are friends. We only want to do what we can to help our village. And we are impatient that Ah Chan is too preoccupied to instruct us in our duties as men. Don't distress yourself with what you've heard. We speak aloud what other people whisper. When you become a bachelor you will get used to it."

Keh rose from the circle. "You speak like my *chichi*," he said to Cuc. He walked away, around the *palapa* and into the forest.

One by one the bachelors rose, leaving, either for the *palapa* or for the village. Tutz rose too. And then Cuc.

"Come see us again," Cuc said to Balam, before turning toward the village.

Without a word Tutz followed, catching up with Cuc in a few steps. Together, they walked side-by-side on the trail.

Balam longed to run after, to join them. But he didn't. It would have made him feel too much like the mute dog who followed his brother around.

Part II

Black from the West

One evening, when he was seven, Balam remembered sitting in the courtyard, poking at a millipede with a stick. He knew millipedes were harmless, but the way they moved seemed dangerous. He killed them when he could—they were good sport and he did not like the thought of their many legs crawling over him in his sleep.

This particular millipede was longer than one of his fingers, and feisty. Its legs waved, looking as if they were fighting among themselves, and it writhed, curling over itself and the stick, rolling this way and that. As the evening light grew dim, Balam found it difficult to see the millipede, to enjoy this play before killing it.

"Balam!"

His *chichi* rushed from the *palapa*.

"It is time! Go tell your father to fetch the midwife. He is visiting with Ah Chan. Go!"

Balam looked up for a second at the agitated face of his *chichi* and nodded. It was time to kill the millipede anyway, to put an end to this play. But when he looked down, the millipede was gone. He looked about, growing frantic, but the shadows were as dark as the undersides of dropped leaves, where millipedes like to hide. It could be anywhere. He shivered, the skin of his back crawling. Or was he feeling the millipede skittering toward his head?

"Did you hear me, boy?"

His grandmother moved toward him, threatening

with a raised arm, when a cry came from inside the *pala-pa*. "Go . . . now!" she growled before lowering her arm and disappearing into the *palapa*.

Balam stood, shaking off the millipede, real or imag-ined. The shaking turned to shivers.

Only moments ago Lord Sun had been disguised in a fluttering cape of yellow and crimson and purple feath-ers as he slipped below the horizon, into Xibalba. With a puff of evening air, the cape had disappeared with him. Balam had never before walked alone in the village at this time of the evening. He was only seven, and unlike the millipede, he didn't find comfort or safety in dark-ness. But Nakin, his stepmother, was about to have a child, and Balam knew he must fetch his father.

The whitewashed, loosely stacked stone wall around his courtyard seemed to glow, like chunks of the moon fallen to earth. The moment he stepped through the wall's gap it felt to Balam as if he, too, were stepping over the edge of the world, slipping into the dark, the cold, the danger of Xibalba, and without the protection of a cape.

It was terrifying. He was torn between moving slow-ly and carefully—so as not to attract the attention of *aluxob*—and hurrying, running. But running might attract the attention of the dangerous creatures that slunk up from Xibalba to do mischief under cover of night. Running would only encourage them to pursue.

Balam had always enjoyed hearing the stories Ah

Chan told of Lord Sun making his way through Xibalba each night, overcoming the trickery and wrath of the Lords of Xibalba so he could rise in the eastern sky each morning, triumphant and splendid, born once more.

But now, removed from the safety of his family, the world around felt like the Xibalba of those stories. His ears twitched at the slightest sounds, causing his scalp to creep across his skull—or was it the millipede? His eyes saw movement, but only at the edges of his vision. He glanced at the stars, shining through leaves, but quickly looked back down—their blinking made them appear too much like the unfriendly eyes of creatures lurking in the tree tops.

As Balam made his way down the path toward the village center, toward Ah Chan's *palapa,* he wondered if Lord Sun was feeling as he felt now. What danger lurked for the god below? How close would he come to perishing before being reborn?

It seemed endless, the path to Ah Chan's *palapa*. But finally he arrived, breathless, momentarily blinded by the light of the small but intense fire around which sat Uk and Ah Chan and several other village men. They were all smiling as broadly as the bowls next to them, empty now of *balche*.

"You must fetch the midwife!"

Uk's smile disappeared and he seemed to rise with the smoke as he stood.

"Go back to the *palapa* and do what you can to help,"

Uk ordered. "I will be there soon." He disappeared into the darkness.

Balam hesitated a moment, not wanting to challenge the night spirits again. And then Ah Chan rose with the smoke, rising and rising, seeming to lift off the ground as his face rose above the small circle of the fire's light. Balam watched, awed, even though he knew it was only Ah Chan's tremendous height that made him seem to float as he stood. "Come," came his godfather's voice from darkness. "I will go with you."

Balam was grateful, but Ah Chan took such long strides that he was barely able to keep up, barely able to keep him within sight in the darkness. As he ran, stumbling, his fear of *aluxob* was replaced by fear for Nakin. His twin brother had died being born, and his mother with him. Just more than a year ago, a child of Nakin's had died being born. Would this baby also die? Would Nakin die?

He could hear the groans and the cries even before he entered the courtyard. Surely that was not a good sign. He watched Ah Chan stoop to enter the *palapa*, but he did not follow. Balam was afraid to enter. Chilled in more than body, he huddled just outside the light that fell through the *palapa* door and buried his face in his knees. Rocking backward and forward, Balam hummed bits of song that Nakin sometimes sang to him. His humming did not keep Nakin's cries and groans from reaching him, but it helped. And when his father arrived with the midwife, rushing past him as if he wasn't there, Balam relaxed enough to fall asleep. But his sleep was troubled, filled with Nakin's distant cries.

н   н   н

The air was so dark, so black, it was hard to breathe. It was cold and it stank—his nose hurt to let it in.

And there were sounds—cries became moans, moans became shrieks. He crawled, hoping to escape the noises and the smells, feeling with his hands a slimy softness, like that of rotten fruit, or flesh. He got up onto his feet and tried to run, but slipped and stumbled—stumbled into something hard, yet covered with a cloth so soft it must have been made of feathers.

"*Wac!*" he heard. And the cloth moved, drawing open, revealing a glowing face, as much like a jaguar's as a man's.

A clawed hand reached out and drew him inside. The air was warm and fresh inside the cape, and Balam breathed deeply. Beside this creature was a large pot, tall as Balam.

"I am Lord Sun," the creature growled. "Do as I command, or I will eat you." He handed Balam a knife, shedding the cape as he did so. The faint light remained around him. "Take hold of my hair and cut off my head," he ordered, kneeling. Bowing, his head hung over the opening of the pot. With trembling hands, Balam placed the knife on the muscled neck. "Quickly," Lord Sun growled.

The knife cut through bone and flesh as though through air. He clutched the hair as blood from the Lord Sun's severed neck surged into the pot, as if vomited. Although it was the darkest blood Balam had ever seen, it seemed to sparkle, as if with *ch'ulel*, as if it contained crumbled bits of stars. When the blood had stopped flowing, he looked to the head, fascinated but dreading what he would see. Calmly, it blinked once and then spoke.

"Place my head within the pot. Next, cut off my arms and legs. Place all my pieces into the pot. There is a wooden plug at your feet. Fit it into the mouth of the pot and tamp it tight. Wrap yourself in my cape and then roll the pot to the river, yonder, and float with it to the east."

Balam did as he was told. With no face to look at, he cut with more confidence, with bolder strokes. And when he rolled the pot to the river he found the water was warm and thick as blood. Instead of weighing him down, pulling him with it into the liquid, the cape floated, spreading out like a flower fallen from a tree onto the *cenote's* water.

The cries and moans grew louder instead of fainter, and he heard a thump, like that of a heart, quiet at first, growing loud enough that he felt it with his entire body. When he felt mud once more under his feet, he rolled the pot up onto shore, and huddled under the cape for protection more than warmth, wondering what to do next. The thumping grew louder still, now seeming to come from the pot itself. A heartbeat? A fist pounding?

As he listened, pondering, a voice came from the calabash, sounding distant and hollow, but unmistakable. "Well done. Take out my pieces, one by one, and lay them in their proper order. When all the pieces are together, I will mend, becoming whole." This Balam did. Standing before him, unsteady and weak, Lord Sun said, "Help me lift the calabash, so that I may drink of my own blood. The *ch'ulel* of my blood will make me strong . . . will make me whole."

As he lifted the calabash to Lord Sun's trembling hands, a voice roared from behind.

"Rascal! We have found you at last!"

"Run!" Lord Sun snarled. "Run fast, so the cape will flutter behind you! Run fast, so they will think you are me!"

Balam ran, the cape seeming to lift him off the ground. He ran from the drumbeat, thumping like his own heart now. He ran from the snarling of his pursuers growing louder and louder, closer and closer. . . .

H   H   H

Balam woke suddenly, completely, out of breath, surrounded by the darkness of night. He was curled up, on his side, still outside the door, trembling from the dream and the cold. He sat up, listening, hearing nothing. Was the silence a good sign? An uneasiness crawled around in his gut, as if the millipede had entered through his mouth or nose while he slept.

He stood stiffly, trying to quiet his breathing, not wanting to disturb the silence, looking to the east. He had escaped Xibalba. But had Lord Sun been as lucky?

He watched the sky with trepidation. Was life possible without Lord Sun? Would maize grow by the light of the moon and stars? Would maize taste bitter, grown by the light of Venus?

As he watched, the sky began to lighten. Slowly, slowly it turned red, like blood through cloth. His trepidation turned to joy. Once more Lord Sun was reborn!

From the *palapa* came an unfamiliar cry. And then Balam knew what it was he was hearing. He rushed inside to see if the new child was a sister or a brother.

FIVE

Balam woke to thumping—the same sound he often heard in his worst dreams. Fearfully, he opened his eyes and was relieved to see light creeping through the *palapa* door, stalking the darkness—once more Lord Sun had survived his trip through Xibalba.

Immediately, embarrassment fell like a shadow over his relief. The thumping must be Ix Bacal grinding breadnuts to paste for making tortillas. What must she think of him, sleeping so late?

His embarrassment became disappointment. This was the day his father was going to start making *holche* at their *milpa*—to chop the underbrush and spread the foliage over the ground so it would dry well and burn easily. This was the day he had planned to show his father he could do a man's work, that he should never again be left behind while important work—men's work—was being done. Judging from the light, his father had already left to work in the coolness of the early morning.

How could he have slept through the noise of everyone getting up? Even Tooch was gone from the *palapa*. And Nakin. The nightmare must have possessed him so utterly that he had not heard the noises of his family stirring. Why hadn't somebody—his *chichi* at least—wakened him? Perhaps the dream had been so strong it had transported his body to Xibalba. Perhaps his father and Nakin and *Chichi* had seen an empty bed and thought he was awake when, in fact, he'd been helping Lord Sun outwit the Lords of Death.

Balam shuddered. Sometimes the world of dreams was more vivid than the world of daylight. Sometimes it was difficult to tell one from the other—as difficult as deciding if the face in the *cenote's* water was his own or his twin brother's. He'd sometimes wondered if his dreams were the waking life of his brother—if his own waking life became the dreams of his brother.

Balam shook these thoughts from his head as he stood, moving to the rhythm of the thump-thump-thump coming from the cooking shed. Next to his bed lay the stout chopping stick, studded with a row of chipped rock, with which he made *holche*. It was not as large as his father's, but it felt good in his hand. Judging by the green stains from cut plants, it worked well and had been well-worked. Walking from the *palapa* he saw Nakin sitting in the courtyard, facing east, braiding lengths of grass into rope for making the sandals he and his father would wear when they burned *holche*.

She looked up from her work, her tired face appearing as if she hadn't slept.

"Good morning," he said, pleased to speak first in the morning, as a man should. Could he see a roundness to her belly? Or was it the way her *huipil* fell forward with her work, or his imagination?

"Good morning," she replied, in a voice that hadn't spoken since waking. "You are late."

"Yes," Balam said. "Why didn't anyone wake me?"

"You were crying out in your sleep. You needed to come back from where you were before you awoke. Otherwise you might have been stuck there forever." And then, looking down at her work, she said, "It is as if we all live in a bad dream from which we cannot wake."

Balam wanted to reassure Nakin, say something that would make her feel better. But his thoughts were interrupted by the laughing shrieks of Tooch, coming from the cooking shed. These shrieks were followed by the lower voice of their *chichi*.

Tooch ran from between the *palapas*, his white bead bouncing wildly around his head, the scrawny dog at his heels. He held something in his hand—what, Balam couldn't tell. Surprised, Tooch paused when he saw Balam and his mother, and then laughed, running behind Nakin, as if for protection. The dog ran to the shadowy edges of the courtyard, away from Balam.

"There is thunder in the cooking shed!" Tooch yelled in mock terror, peering around his mother to where their *chichi* now stood.

"Yes," she rumbled. "And where there is thunder, rain is sure to follow." She stepped forward and Tooch sprang sideways, preparing to run away. Quick as Tooch was, Balam's leg was quicker. His half-brother landed on both knees and his one empty hand. Dark spots appeared in the dirt as sudden tears spilled from Tooch's eyes.

"*Chichi*, look! Mother, look!" Balam bent over his brother. "Rain marking the dirt!" He smiled as he helped Tooch stand. "Go water the garden, where rain is truly needed," he said, letting go of his arm.

With Tooch gone, his *chichi* turned toward Balam. "If you hadn't slept so late, Tooch would not have been able to steal away some of the food I made for you to take to the *milpa*."

She turned, stomping off, disappearing in the direction of the cooking shed.

Balam sighed. He looked at Nakin and shrugged his shoulders. "Maybe I should have stayed in the place of my dreams," he said, pleased at the twitch of a smile that almost awakened her mouth.

In the cooking shed, Balam saw Ix Bacal grinding, the paste of breadnuts coating her hands to her wrists. Gone was the gracefulness with which she'd moved yesterday. She seemed to attack the paste as if she were angry.

Thump-thump-thump. *Thump*-thump-*thump!*

And then came the growl of his *chichi's* voice. She was bent over her *opps,* tending a tortilla. "If it hadn't been for you and your fish, it wouldn't have happened!"

Ix Bacal flinched at *Chichi's* words. Looking at Balam, anger smoldered in her eyes. Abruptly, her gaze shifted to the far edge of the cooking shed, near the *opps.* Balam let his eyes travel there also.

The iguana lay on its back, its legs stiff and reaching upward. It was dead, and had been for some time. How could that be?

His *chichi* rose from her work and turned to Balam and Ix Bacal. "Yes," she said, her voice hard with anger. "It died sometime during the night and is now spoiled for eating. Perhaps the *yum kaax* poisoned it! Perhaps it swallowed its own tongue . . . I don't know! Take it and its evil with you and throw it into the forest on your way to the *milpa*," she said, handing Balam several tortillas and a packet of food for later.

And then she turned to Ix Bacal. "We need for you to fetch water . . . now! And don't bring back any fish with it!"

Balam glanced at Ix Bacal. Along with anger, he now saw fear. Did he see fear of his *chichi*, or of fetching water?

H   H   H

As he hurried toward the *milpa*, he couldn't banish the angry, fearful look on Ix Bacal's face from his mind. The iguana had stiffened in death and was easy to carry, and to throw. As soon as he had tossed it into the forest he turned back, running toward the village and the trail that led to the *cenote*. What must she think of him, not coming to her defense when his *chichi* had been so unfair? Was it right for him to be afraid of his *chichi's* anger? If he was almost a man, shouldn't he have defended his future wife?

He saw her ahead, almost to the *cenote,* and sped up. He hoped she would be pleased he'd come to help. Upon hearing the sound of his running she spun around, her mouth gaping, surprised, unpleasantly so.

"It's *me!*" Balam slowed to a walk.

Modestly, she closed her mouth and looked away from him, stepping off to the side for him to pass. Did she think he was passing this way on another errand?

"No, Ix Bacal," he said. "I've come to help you." Gently, he took the calabash from her.

She glanced at him, and Balam was glad to see that what he'd done pleased her.

There was no need for words. Her silence, and the way in which she walked just behind, told him she considered him a man. His chest seemed to swell with each breath as he walked ahead of her to the edge of the *cenote*. It felt somehow dangerous to be completely alone with Ix Bacal, and wonderful. There was so much he wanted to say. But he wanted to act as a man would act, to speak only of important things, not chatter like a child in her presence.

Balam tried to appear more confident than he felt as

he threw the *cenote's* calabash over the edge. Ah Chan had purified its water—pouring *balche* into it, followed by a figure carved in jade, and songs and prayers. Even with this knowledge, Balam found himself watchful and uneasy as he pulled water from the *cenote* and then poured it into his *chichi's* calabash. He poured carefully, slowly, watching the thin ribbon stretch from one calabash to the other, watching for the lumpy shadows of fish in the water. He saw nothing to knot the ribbon.

With the large calabash filled, Balam looked up at Ix Bacal. She was so beautiful! He felt proud that she was to be his wife.

"There are no fish in this water. I must go now to work with my father," he said, helping settle the calabash on Ix Bacal's head.

Turning, feeling suddenly shy, he ran—back to the village, past *palapas* and the plaza, out into the forest, to his father's *milpa*.

⋈   ⋈   ⋈

As Lord Sun trudged across the sky, the day grew hotter and hotter. Balam worked hard alongside his father, hoping to make up for being late. He was grateful that his father had merely nodded a greeting when he arrived, not asking why he was late, or punishing him.

It pleased Balam to think his father might believe that whatever his reason for being late, it was worthy. It pleased him to think his father might see that he was too old to be treated as a boy, even if he was not yet a man.

The pride he felt gave him renewed energy as he made *holche*. He chopped at the undergrowth, struggling to keep pace with his father, feeling sweat slide from his hair and down his face. As he worked, Balam stole sideways glances and was relieved to see sweat also glistened on his father's forehead, which sloped more steeply than his nose. Balam hoped his own forehead, shaped by cradle boards shortly after he was born, was as handsome, as steeply sloped as his father's. Balam hoped he would grow to be as strong and graceful as his father.

Last year he and his father had cleared this *milpa* for the first time. Never before had Balam helped his father with such work. They had cut wide, deep rings through the bark of trees too large to chop down, rings that strangled and killed. These large trees were partly burned through from last year and, being long dead, were better for burning this year than last. In the meantime, the undergrowth had grown back—encouraged by the light let in through the naked trees, only slightly stunted, seeming to defy the drought. As they worked, the cleared *milpa* grew toward the forest's edge.

Lord Sun grew hot as he toiled upward and across the sky, casting off heat, the steam of his sweat thickening the air. The hotter Lord Sun became, the hotter Balam became. Sweat dropped off him like the rain he hoped would come soon. Balam hoped that the *itz* of his sweat would help the maize grow. *Itz* was powerful, the stuff of life, found within secretions from living things—

in milk and the sap of trees, in tears and semen, in the nectar of flowers. Rain contained the *itz* of the Chac gods and, from rain, maize gathered *itz*. It was from maize that people gathered this spirit, to live side-by-side with *ch'ulel* in the blood.

Balam imagined he tasted the *itz* in his sweat as its saltiness crept through the corners of his mouth. A bead of sweat slipped into his right eye and he paused, blinking. The blurriness slowly disappeared as he peered about the *milpa*. Soon he could clearly see its square shape, aligned to each direction as was the village plaza, marked by piles of rocks at the corners and sides. Unlike the plaza, in the *milpa's* center there was no ceiba tree, only three stones arranged in a triangle, like his *chichi's* hearthstones, like the three stones of creation at the center of the heavens, where the gods started the first fire.

Hoping to see clouds, he glanced over his shoulder to the east, the direction of red, where Lord Sun was born each morning. It was from the east that the clouds of *hahah* came, laden with rain that gave birth to maize. He saw only clear sky.

What was keeping the rain? Were the Chac gods so weak they could not send rain? Didn't they know the rain was for their own well-being? Rain meant maize and maize fed the men who in turn fed the gods. The spiral flow of *itz* from the gods to people and back to the gods was in danger of being broken.

Sighing, he noticed silence had replaced the rhythmic chop-chop-chop of his father's cutting stick. Embarrassed, Balam saw his father standing still, staring at him.

"Listening to the chatter of monkeys in your head?" his father asked. On his face was a small, tight smile.

"Yes," Balam replied, encouraging his father's smile with one of his own.

When his father tilted his head to one side, Balam sensed his question just before it was uttered. "What caused you to be late this morning?"

Balam hesitated, feeling foolish for thinking his father wouldn't ask about his tardiness, for thinking his father would assume he had a worthy, grown-up reason for being late.

"I woke late," he said, feeling his face grow as red as the dawn he should have seen but didn't. Should he tell of helping Ix Bacal with the water?

"I thought I heard your *chichi's* scolding all the way out here." Uk smiled, knowingly.

Balam nodded. "Was *Chichi* always so angry when you were a boy?"

Uk seemed surprised by this question. "No. But she can rail at people more easily than at the gods. She must scold someone, and we are handy." He glanced up. "The new day has come. Let's eat what your *chichi* has prepared for us."

Together they walked to the edge of the forest. From the branch of a small tree hung a small calabash. In a crotch of the tree rested the packets of food for Uk and Balam.

"Your meal seems lighter to me than usual," Uk said, handing Balam his food.

"Tooch took some of my food while I slept." His father nodded.

They ate in silence. As he ate, Balam tried to remember the taste of maize. He could not.

ᴴ   ᴴ   ᴴ

Long before Lord Sun approached the tops of the trees to the west of the *milpa,* they were startled by the cries of Tooch running toward them.

"Father! Father!"

Both Uk and Balam straightened their aching backs and watched the boy run closer. What could be wrong? Would there ever be a day without crisis? Or was Tooch having fun, pretending there was a crisis when there was not?

"Ah Chan wants to speak with you!"

Uk nodded, as if he'd been expecting this news. He turned to Balam. "Continue without me."

Before Balam could say anything Uk was gone. Tooch lingered for a moment, gazing about the *milpa* hopefully. By the change in his face, Balam could tell that his younger brother seemed to decide making *holche* didn't look very exciting. "Good-bye," Tooch shouted, running after his father.

Balam worked at a furious pace, more determined

than ever to impress his father. Step, chop-chop. Step, chop-chop.

Just before stepping, Balam heard a shrill buzzing at his feet. He turned to stone, his cutting stick above his head, his eyes searching the ground for a snake. The rattling grew louder, drawing his eyes toward movement.

The snake was as thick as a braided rope, coiling itself. Its head was raised, tongue flicking, its mouth opened enough so its fangs were unfolding. The rattles were a blur of motion, a blur of sound.

Balam didn't move, didn't breathe. He tightened his grip on the chopping stick and lowered it slightly. He pictured himself moving as quickly as the snake's tongue.

And then the snake struck. Bellowing and jumping, Balam swung. Incredibly, the snake hit wood and fell back, stunned and silent—but only for a moment. As the snake began to gather itself again, the buzz grew more angry than before. Without thinking, Balam brought the stick back and, closing his eyes with effort, he swung— hoping to stop the noise and the fangs and the coiling.

The noise stopped. Had he killed the snake? Balam took a couple of ragged breaths before opening his eyes. What he saw surprised him. At his feet lay a set of rattles. He heard rustling as the snake retreated through the undergrowth.

As if in a dream, Balam picked up the rattles. The rattles of a snake were good luck. But what luck was it to have rattles with a snake crawling through the *milpa*—its fangs filled with venom, wounded and angry, silent and able to strike without warning?

He searched for the snake, looking for a tell-tale trail of blood, carefully poking at the underbrush with his chopping stick. Finally, he gave up and continued to work.

He worked until Lord Sun began sliding toward Xibalba, his brilliant cloak catching for a moment on the tree tops. As he worked, Balam kept the rattles in one hand, hoping their luck would overcome the danger of having a rattlesnake nearby that couldn't give warning before it struck.

SIX

Balam's stomach growled as he walked through the courtyard. If only he'd had more to eat during the day, he might have gotten more done. He swung his right arm back and forth, proud of the way it felt—larger, more muscled. Would anyone notice? He tried striding like a man, letting the rattles in his hand make muffled noise.

Nakin was in the courtyard, still braiding grass. Had she been braiding all day? She looked up as Balam strode toward her. Her smile was not one of somebody who'd been braiding all day.

"Look," he said, holding out the rattles, hoping they would impress her. "I cut these off a snake in the *milpa*."

Her eyes grew large.

Balam handed them to her. "This is for our altar. I hope it will bring us good luck."

He waited for her to thank him. But before she could

say anything, he heard his *chichi's* voice coming from the cooking shed.

"Balam?" How had she known it was he? Surely he hadn't spoken loudly enough for her to hear. Perhaps he smelled like his father after working hard. His father's smell often traveled ahead, with a loudness all its own, greeting people before he was in sight. "Balam. Come here."

He walked between the *palapas* to the cooking shed. His *chichi* was bent over her *opps,* hovering, poking at the fire.

"I'm out of wood," she said without turning around.

Was she asking him to fetch wood at the end of the day, after working in the *milpa*? Why hadn't she ordered Tooch to fetch wood?

"Where's Tooch?" he asked, suspecting that Tooch had noticed the need for wood and made himself scarce.

Just then, as if summoned by Balam's question, Tooch burst into the cooking shed, followed closely by the dog.

"Balam!" he cried happily. "I almost caught a macaw with my hands!" As proof he held up a long red feather.

"Get that dog out of here!" barked *Chichi*. At the sound of her voice, the dog slunk into shadows.

Tooch spun around, facing his *chichi,* waving the feather in front of her face. "Look, *Chichi*! See! I almost caught a macaw! You said I would never catch one. But I almost did!"

Their *chichi* looked past the feather, directly into Tooch's face. "Go with Balam. Help him fetch wood for the fire."

H   H   H

"The macaw was big, like this. . . ." Tooch spread his arms apart to show Balam how big.

Balam refused to smile. He knew how much Tooch wanted to catch a macaw and keep it to pluck long feathers from its wings and tail—enough, certainly, to make up stories. But keeping and feeding a macaw would be more trouble than it was worth. These days, who could buy feathers, even the beautiful feathers of a macaw?

He glanced at the feather. How easy it would be for Tooch to have picked a feather from the ground, plucked by a preening bird, and then claim he'd pulled it from a bird that had barely escaped. "Show me the feather," he demanded.

Tooch hesitated, suspecting his older brother of a trick. "You don't believe me," he said.

"How can I believe if you don't show me the feather? Maybe it isn't even the feather of a macaw. Maybe it's the feather of a snake."

"Snakes don't have . . ." Tooch caught himself, realizing a moment too late that he was being teased. In some ways he was very much like his mother. Reluctantly, Tooch handed the feather to Balam.

Balam turned the feather over in his hands. Indeed, it was a macaw feather, and it was clean. It was not smudged with dirt from having fallen to the ground. On the quill end was attached a shred of skin, showing it had been just recently pulled from a bird.

Was it possible that his younger brother had, truly, almost caught a macaw, even with that dog—barkless as it was—for a shadow?

"Tell me the story of the feather." Balam handed the feather back, trying to sound as if he was doing his brother a favor to listen. He stooped to pick up a fat stick from alongside the path, probably fallen from the bundle of somebody trudging back to the village. He walked into the forest where deadfall was plentiful. "Can you talk and pick up wood at the same time?"

"Of course," Tooch said, grabbing a stick almost too small for a bird to notice. "I have been watching a macaw in the great ceiba tree for many days . . . watching how it stayed in the tree until it saw food to steal. And for many days now I have been putting a little food out for it . . . food I saved from the evening meal . . . from the afternoon meal. And each time I would get a little closer to the food so the macaw would grow to trust me. And this morning, with more food than usual. . . ."

Tooch closed his mouth with a snap. By now Balam had an armful of wood. He turned to look at his brother and saw in the young boy's face something he was not supposed to see. What had happened this morning began to take on a different meaning.

"It was *my* food you used today, wasn't it! *My* food

you stole to feed a macaw!" He wanted to grab Tooch and shake him. He made a move to do just that when the wood shifted in his arms, threatening to fall. There was fear in Tooch's face.

But Tooch's fear turned to glee when he realized Balam couldn't catch him and carry wood at the same time. "Yes," Tooch said, giggling nervously. "And I almost got the macaw! I did! And I think you believe me now!" He danced away, jumping while he thrust the feather into the air. The dog danced too, jumping toward the feather in Tooch's hand.

Angry as he was, Balam couldn't help himself. He smiled. He would never have guessed that his brother possessed the wile or patience to almost catch a macaw.

"No," he said. "I *don't* believe you. I believe the macaw trained you to bring it food so that someday it could get close enough to peck out your eyes . . . and the eyes of that dog, too."

Tooch turned to grin at Balam, to say something insulting. The dog jumped into the air and came down with the feather in its mouth. Tooch shrieked. The terrified dog bolted into the forest.

"Come back!" Tooch shouted, beginning to cry. "Come back!"

Balam sighed. "Gather wood, little brother, or *Chichi* will give you more to cry about than a lost feather."

◼ ◼ ◼

Balam and Tooch returned to the *palapa* just as darkness began to rise from the ground, filling the sky like *cenote* water fills a calabash from the bottom up. Without the feather, Tooch had been able to gather a respectable amount of wood. The dog was waiting for him, the feather in its mouth—a little wet but otherwise unharmed.

Uk was still not back from wherever he'd gone, even after Balam bathed off the man smell. *Chichi* fed them anyway. Balam was surprised and pleased that his *chichi* treated him with the respect she usually showed only toward his father—serving him first, keeping her face turned down and away from him, staying just out of sight while he ate. Also, she was silent. Balam found it pleasant to eat without being scolded, but found himself wondering what thoughts and feelings his *chichi* was hiding behind the silence. Had Nakin told her about the rattles?

Uk still had not returned after Balam finished eating. After his day of work, Balam was tired. Nakin had already gone to bed, and Balam walked into the darkened *palapa* as quietly as he could.

Tired as he was, Balam slept fitfully. His dreams were full of fear and unpleasantness, the same dreams that had troubled him when he was younger. When his eyes flew open, his heart pounding, it was still dark. Feeling caught between his dreams and wakefulness, he got up from his bed and crept toward the *palapa* door.

The old fears that had haunted him when he was seven were present, clear as the forest shadows that made fallen trees look like human bodies, vines look like snakes, bodies and snakes that twisted as the shadows shifted. Perhaps nothing was what it appeared to be. Perhaps he, Balam, wasn't fourteen, but just a seven-year-old boy who merely had dreamed of growing older. It was easy to imagine such a thing in the darkness before dawn.

He looked to the east, squatting, watching as the sky changed. A great band of stars, crowded together, stretched across the sky. Those stars paved the White Road of heaven, the Great *Sacbe*, the road with its portal to the Underworld. The heavenly *sacbe* was fading, spreading thin, smearing the sky with a shallow light.

As Lord Sun rose from Xibalba, Balam stood and began to shiver.

"Cold?" came his father's quiet voice from behind.

The warmth of his father's hand, resting now on his shoulder, caused him to shiver even more. "Yes."

His father squeezed gently, knowingly. "It is a wonder that Lord Sun survives every night. I too am sometimes fearful he will not be born again . . . that we will have to live forever in darkness."

Balam had never heard his father speak of such a fear before. It was at once reassuring and frightening. There were times when Balam looked forward to manhood, hoping that he would become strong enough, wise enough, to leave his fears behind. But the drought had taken its toll, revealing fears in Ah Chan and in his father he'd never suspected were there all along—fears almost like those of women, like Nakin's and his *chichi's*. What other fears did his father dress in manly silence, like an *ex* wrapped nervously, too tight? When he was a man, Balam knew he too would be expected to hide his fears, just as he would be expected to hide his manhood. Would his fears ever go away?

His father lifted his hand. The morning air felt like a cold rock resting where it had been warm only an instant before. "Where did you go, when you left the *milpa*?" Balam turned to face his father.

His father stared, his face growing more distinct as the sunlight grew stronger. From behind his father came the groans and sighs of his family waking.

"There are too many ears to hear my answer," his father answered.

"And there are too many answers for my ears to hear," growled *Chichi* as she pushed past them both, on her way to the cooking shed.

Balam returned his father's smile with one of his own. "Some ears hear only more questions when an answer is given," said Uk, loudly enough for his mother to hear.

Balam was pleased to see Ix Bacal arrive just a moment after his *chichi* went to wake the fire that slumbered between the three rocks of her hearth. He wanted to linger, to watch Ix Bacal work, to be near her—to catch her glancing at him, perhaps—but soon he was following his father along the path to the *milpa*.

He found himself longing to help Ix Bacal fetch water, yet wanting to be with his father. His feet carried him along toward the *milpa* while his heart raced back, pounding with effort, to be with his future wife.

Just before they arrived, both Balam and his father turned to the sound of footsteps running toward them. The man, Keh's father, stopped several armlengths from them and beckoned to Uk. Uk stepped toward him and cocked his head to listen to the man's whispering.

Uk straightened, his face troubled, and turned toward Balam. "I must go. Work hard." His words were as abrupt as his leaving.

H   H   H

Balam hung his food and water from a young tree and began to work, methodically stepping and chopping, stepping and chopping. Yesterday his right arm had felt larger, more muscled. Today it felt sore and was difficult to lift. He shifted his chopping stick to his left hand as often as he could, but he could barely control the swings of that arm, once almost hitting himself in the head.

Whenever he found himself lulled by the monotonous rhythm of chopping, he pictured the snake from yesterday and his mind sprang to wakefulness. Was the snake lurking in the underbrush ahead?

Balam worked until he could barely lift his arm. When he finally allowed himself to rest, Balam was surprised to see Lord Sun had climbed to the top of the sky and was now going down. What could be keeping his father?

Balam scanned the *milpa*. Hard as he had worked, there was so much left to do! Discouraged, he walked to the tree where his food and water hung. As he squatted to eat, he watched a turtle walk across the cleared area of the *milpa,* going from east to west. It had been a long time since he'd seen a turtle walking about, slow and steady, but with purpose and patience. Balam could not help considering the turtle a good sign. It was on the shell of a turtle that the earth floated up from the time when nothing existed but water. It was from the split shell of a turtle that the Maize God, First Father, was reborn. And it was the rumble of turtle shell drums that sounded like distant thunder, calling to the Chacs, to the clouds. Yes, this turtle was undoubtedly a good sign. Was it a messenger from the Red Chac of the east, the direction from which rain came? If so, what was the message?

Once more he wished his father were here to answer this question. Was the turtle's message a warning? Or did the turtle bring good news—at long last?

He finished his food and went back to work. He was so lost in the chop-step, chop-step of making *holche* it took him a few moments to realize his father was next to him, matching him blow for blow. Balam wanted to greet his father, talk with him about the snake and the turtle, to ask where his father had been. Just in time he caught the strong smells of tobacco and *balche*. His father must have been with Ah Chan and other men of the village, talking among themselves and trying to converse with the gods.

As much as his father stank of tobacco and *balche,* he worked as fast and as hard as yesterday. In the little time they had left in the afternoon, Balam and his father made enormous progress. His father worked like a madman, not chopping undergrowth so much as seeming to chop at demons emerging from the ground, coming from Xibalba.

SEVEN

They worked in silence, his father seemingly unaware that Lord Sun's shimmering cloak was shredding on the topmost branches of trees to the west.

"Father," Balam said in a voice he used to wake somebody. "It's time for us to go."

The skin around Uk's eyes looked bruised, as if from a fight. Without a word he lowered his chopping stick. Turning, he walked toward the village, shoulders hunched, head down.

Quickly, Balam studied the *milpa*. How could his father have been so tired, yet worked so hard? They'd made tremendous progress since his father came—there was little left to do. One person, he thought, does the work of one. Two people working separately do the work of two. But two people working together sometimes do the work of three . . . or four.

When he turned to go, Balam saw his father standing

at the far end of the *milpa*, at the forest's edge. Was his father waiting for help? Companionship? Instead, as Balam approached, he saw his father was merely staring beyond, into the *milpa*. His eyes flicked back and forth, as if he were seeing animals or people moving here and there. "We have wounded the forest . . . killed part of it," he said, finally shifting his eyes toward Balam. The darks of his watery eyes continued to flick back and forth, floating like two struggling flies in *balche*. "Life comes from the taking of life."

When he turned to walk away, Balam followed, puzzling over his father's words. The words themselves did not puzzle him—they were true enough. But there had been something unusual in the way his father said those words. There had been something in the way his father had looked at him. With a sense of uneasiness, Balam felt his father had been speaking of his mother's death as she had given birth to him.

H   H   H

The next morning, Balam once more rose before everyone else. Pleased with himself, he crept from the *palapa*, taking only a sticky lump of ground breadnut, big as his fist, and a small calabash of water. Later he would make a cold gruel to help him with his day's work.

He ran to the *milpa*, holding the chopping stick off to the side so it wouldn't cut him if he tripped and fell. The forest was quiet. The world seemed uneasy, caught between dreams and waking. Finally, to Balam's relief, birds began to call as light spread across the sky, thin and watery, causing the darkness to shimmer.

At the *milpa,* Balam quickly broke up the ground breadnut, crumbling bits into the water. Placing his palm over the calabash's opening, he shook. Drinking some of this gruel, he wished he'd remembered to put honey in the water. But then, honey was becoming as precious, as scarce, as maize. There were few flowers and most bees had stopped flying, instead gathering together in their hives, huddling in lumps that covered their dwindling combs, humming instead of buzzing, eating little as they waited for *hahah* and the return of flowers. Because of this his *chichi* guarded her honey with unusual ferocity. Of course, Nakin had used hers long ago.

He worked hard, attacking the undergrowth with such energy he grunted each time he swung the chopping stick. *Grunt*-chop-step! Grunt-*chop*-step! *Grunt-chop*-step! He wanted to finish before his father arrived, as a gift to his father and as a proof to himself he could work like a man. He was hopeful he could finish before the new day began.

His movements and the noises he made were hypnotic. Soon, it seemed as if the chopping stick worked separately from him, doing the work itself, dragging his arm along behind. It was as if he was becoming the air he breathed. With each breath he felt lighter, more like air than flesh—air with smells strong enough to see, smells strong enough perhaps to be a man's.

"You have done well."

Balam was startled from his trance by these words, spoken quietly but seeming to boom with the force of drumbeats in the quiet of the *milpa*. He looked up, his eyes so unfocused that his father reminded him of a reflection on *cenote* water. His father's face sharpened as he smiled, his eyes tired but the skin around them almost clear of bruises.

Balam felt cheated. Work in the *milpa* was nearly done and now he would be unable to finish this gift for his father.

These feelings must have shown on his face. "I can see the work on our *milpa* is in good hands. In any case, I am needed elsewhere." He handed Balam a packet of food wrapped in leaves. "Nakin was afraid you had walked into the forest in your sleep, called by whatever evil things from Xibalba trouble your dreams. But your *chichi* told her such fear was nonsense . . . and went to the cooking shed and made you something to eat."

Balam smiled. "Would you let me share this with you?"

Uk shook his head. "I am fasting, Balam. We will burn our *milpas* in seven days and I wish to be pure so the Chacs will listen to my prayer."

Balam took the food but did not open it. If his father was fasting, he wanted to fast. "I will work some more before I eat," he said, not knowing if his father would be pleased or not about his fasting.

Abruptly, his father turned and strode off. Why was there so much awkwardness between them lately? Why did it seem as if dust filled their heads in the same way dust often filled the air lately? Only after his father was gone did Balam realize that he had been carrying a spear instead of a chopping stick.

H   H   H

It had only been three days since he'd been with the boys, but to Balam it seemed much longer. They treated him politely enough, but as they would treat a stranger, not the boy who was their leader.

It was as if they had come to his family's *palapa* not to fetch him, but to fetch Tooch. As they followed him along the trail going to the village center, they made no noise, did not talk. It was as if they were now shy in his presence. The silence was unusual, uncomfortably so. Over his shoulder Balam called, "Let's go to the place where I found the iguana . . . to the ruins. Surely there are more iguanas where I caught that one the other day."

He looked over his shoulder, expecting to see excitement in the faces of the boys. To his surprise, all he saw were faces looking down at shuffling feet—and silence.

"We can't," Tooch finally said, frowning as he looked up.

Balam stopped and turned around, facing them. What was happening? Was his leadership, his authority, being challenged? And by his own half-brother?

"I will go without you, then," Balam said, anger making his words feel like smoke leaving his mouth.

Again Tooch broke the awkward silence. "You can't go either."

Balam glared at Tooch. "And why not?" He took a threatening step toward the boy, who took several steps back. The boys drew closer together, as if for protection.

Tooch tried to sound brave. "Haven't you heard? There are men from the villages all around spying on us . . . lurking in the forest . . . wanting to capture boys or girls . . . or men and women to barter for our maize seed."

Balam squinted at Tooch. If this were true, why hadn't anyone told him before now? Why hadn't his father told him?

"We have been told to stay close to the plaza and the ceiba tree," Tooch said. "And no one may go to the *cenote* alone . . . or without weapons."

Balam thought of the *milpa* and the spear his father had carried instead of a chopping stick. And his words, "I am needed elsewhere." And he had not returned to their *palapa* last night.

Suddenly what he had felt yesterday seemed silly, childish. He had been pleased when his father let him finish making *holche* by himself. Looking at the finished *milpa* had made him proud. He had been pleased, thinking that his father accepted the gift of his work, the gift of his manhood. But now he realized his father had other reasons for letting him finish clearing the *milpa*. His father might even have been hiding in the forest around the *milpa,* guarding him from spies and raiders. Had he been left working as bait to attract the enemies of his village?

These boys had known more than he about what was happening! Balam felt humiliated as he looked at Tooch's face. When Balam looked at the other faces, he saw smirks and stares that told him they no longer held him in the same regard as before. It had been a while since he'd felt part of them and he remembered the times he'd wanted to cast them out of his life. Instead, these boys had cast him out of their lives, did not trust or like him, did not consider him one of them anymore.

Anger grew inside him. No. He was not a boy any longer. He did not want to spend time with them now. And still he was not a man. He could not yet take his place among men either.

He glared at Tooch. "Make sure the boys stay by the ceiba tree. And stay together. I wouldn't want any ants to carry you off. Don't move, don't cry, don't talk until I come back. I have important work to do . . . work that monkeys cannot do . . . and I don't know when I'll be back."

"We aren't monkeys!" Tooch shouted, his face growing red with anger.

As a group, the boys rushed toward Balam. They meant to harm him.

Balam stood for a moment, determined to fight them if necessary. But even a man would have trouble fighting all of them at once. He felt terrible, almost cowardly, as he turned and began running.

"I would hate to hurt you, little ones," he called over his shoulder.

He heard frustrated, breathless shouting behind. "Coward!" "Monkey!" "Bachelor!"

As he ran, Balam knew. There was only one place he felt he might belong.

H   H   H

Balam did not creep up to the bachelor *palapa* or hide behind the clump of pumpwood bushes. He walked into the courtyard boldly, wanting to belong, wanting to show the other bachelors that he belonged.

He was disappointed to see no bachelors about. Where could they be?

He squatted near the door to their *palapa,* listening and wondering. And as he wondered, he looked about. Someday soon he would come here to live. Someday soon this would be his home, if only for a year, or two or three.

Balam saw an upright pole of the *palapa* leaning away from the others. Should he fix it while he waited? As he tried to decide, he found himself wondering if he would ever feel comfortable living here. He had never slept away from his family—from Nakin and his *chichi.* And he found it difficult to remember the time before Tooch. It was true his father sometimes left for several nights at a time, like last night, but his absence always seemed to draw the rest of the family closer together, as if for comfort.

And, Balam thought, I've never slept so far away from my mother and twin brother.

He looked up with a start as Keh walked into the courtyard.

"What are you doing here?" he asked. His voice and face were unfriendly.

Balam pretended the question did not bother him. He stood, wondering how to answer. Certainly he didn't want to tell Keh that he was at the bachelor *palapa* because he didn't know where else to be—because he was no longer welcome in the company of the boys— because he didn't feel that his father trusted him enough to share what was happening in the village.

Instead of answering Keh's question, he asked one of his own. "Where is Tutz?"

Keh eyed him, critically. "With the other bachelors," he said.

"And where are the other bachelors?" Balam asked.

"With Tutz." Keh smiled at his own cleverness.

Balam smiled too, so that Keh would think he also appreciated Keh's cleverness. But as he smiled he looked at how Keh's head had been shaped unevenly. The boards had been tied crookedly or had slipped, and one side of his forehead sloped back less than the other. Such ugliness was hard to overlook.

"Don't treat him like a stranger!"

Both Balam and Keh turned to see Tutz and Cuc walk into the courtyard with several other bachelors. All of them carried spears.

"Soon he will be one of us," Tutz said. "And he is my brother."

Keh stepped toward Tutz. "If he is your brother, take him back to his mother where he belongs. Perhaps that is where you belong also."

Cuc squatted and drew lines in the courtyard dirt with a stick. He sounded bored. "I think we have enough to fight without fighting each other," he said. "Besides, we have work to do. Ah Chan has told us to patrol the forest between here and the *cenote* for spies," he said. He looked at Balam and then at Tutz.

"I think Balam should join us," Tutz said.

Keh laughed. "What! A boy? Wouldn't he be too scared?"

Tutz's face hardened. "He will soon enough live among us. And," Tutz's voice grew hard, "he is my brother."

Cuc stood. "Must I say it again? We must not fight like this among ourselves. If Balam wants to join us, I say he may."

Balam looked about. Bachelor heads were nodding, some of them looking at Balam and some of them looking at the ground. Nobody looked toward Keh, except Balam. He found Keh staring at him, his mouth set straight and grim.

"If he comes I will not let him slow me down, or

cause danger to follow me," Keh said. Balam knew Keh would never agree to let him join the bachelors today. What he'd just said was as close to permission as Balam was likely to get.

Tutz and Balam smiled at each other. It had been a long time since they'd done anything together. Balam thought of all the times he and Tutz had fought imaginary enemies and jaguars, had tried to catch iguanas, had tried to climb higher than the other in trees, and on the blocks of stone of the old ruined temple.

It felt right to be with Tutz again, even if Keh was not welcoming. It felt right for him to be part of something that was important for the entire village.

"Here." Tutz handed Balam an old chopping stick. "You may need this." It wasn't a spear, but a proud grin grabbed hold of Balam's mouth and wouldn't let go.

EIGHT

It was as dark outside the *palapa* as inside. Darkness seemed to make the air too heavy for morning breezes to stir. As he trudged alongside his father on the path toward the *milpa*, Balam felt hindered by the darkness, as if he were struggling to swing his feet through dew-soaked undergrowth instead of air.

Balam seldom arose from bed this early and his tired thoughts struggled to keep up with his feet. He was tired from rising so early, but it was more than that. He'd been fasting for seven days, drinking only water, and he had difficulty concentrating—sleep interrupted his wakefulness and wakefulness interrupted his sleep.

His father's white *ex* seemed to float all by itself in the darkness ahead. He had followed many an *ex* in the past few days—crouching low through forest undergrowth or scrambling up trees to spy. As he followed his father's *ex*, Balam thought of the things he'd done with the bachelors.

Most of it had been uneventful. They had spent their days patrolling the forest, watching for signs of intruders—spies—kidnappers. The thrill for Balam had come from just being part of them, even though Tutz and Cuc were the only ones who addressed him with the respect of an equal—and then not all the time. The bachelors had accepted him enough to grudgingly let him be with them, even though they expected him to leave each evening, to go back to his own *palapa,* his own family.

The sameness of the days had been broken by one event. Balam smiled as he remembered. On the third day they had split into three groups, intending to surround the *cenote* and work their way inward, trapping any intruder who might have been biding his time, waiting for someone to fetch water. Balam had been with Tutz, Keh, and Cuc. As they made their way toward the *cenote,* through a part of the forest that was tangled with tendrils, Keh bent down, stopping so quickly that Balam almost bumped into him.

"Look," Keh whispered, pointing to the ground.

Cuc and Tutz bent so low Balam couldn't see what Keh pointed to. But when Tutz straightened his back, his mouth was crooked with a smile. "Tracks . . . of a man," he whispered. "Going that way." He pointed to his right.

More quietly than ever, they had followed these tracks looping away from the *cenote,* back to where they had come from. Balam listened carefully for any unusual sounds of movement in the forest. But now, alerted to possible danger, every sound, every movement seemed unusual.

He was the first to see the back of a man's head, low in the undergrowth, his hair pulled up and tied so that it fell like the tassles of maize, black instead of golden. Balam had tugged at Tutz's *ex* and pointed. It looked as if the man, whoever he was, was napping—his head tilted to the side, almost resting on one shoulder.

Carefully, barely daring to breathe, the three bachelors and Balam crawled up behind this figure. Balam had not been able to see any more of the stranger—branches and leaves hid him. Cuc rose first, shouting, and the others followed his lead, brandishing their weapons. The stranger's head jerked up and he stood, turning toward them at the same time, horror showing on his face.

Instead of a stranger, they'd found themselves facing Cantul.

Cantul's surprise had been so great that a yellow stain spread over the front of his *ex*. When he saw who they were he seemed unable to stop talking, telling them that he had been part of a group of bachelors following tracks also and had been concentrating so hard he soon found himself separated from the other men. He'd stopped, sitting, trying to decide what to do.

"But you were sleeping," Keh had said, reproachfully.

"I was thinking and it is hot . . ." Cantul muttered, searching the ground about his feet as if for a better explanation.

"Thinking too much can make a person weary," said Tutz, laughing.

"Especially you, Cantul," said Cuc. There was fondness in his voice. Cantul had smiled, meekly, gratefully.

Balam giggled, remembering this. His father looked back, puzzled. Balam swallowed the remaining giggles. His father turned forward, increasing his pace. Balam hurried more, wanting to keep up with his father and also wanting to keep up with the remembered story playing in his head.

"Weren't you afraid a spy would find you and take you away?" Keh had asked, scolding.

"No," Cantul admitted. And then a stubborn look crossed his face. "There are no men lurking in the forest." Tutz and Cuc grunted their agreement. Grudgingly, even Keh had to admit there probably weren't.

That evening the bachelors had gathered, tired and grumbling among themselves, wondering if perhaps all the talk of spies had been invented by Ah Chan to keep them preoccupied, to keep them too busy to think about the old man's impotence in confronting the drought.

Should I have spoken up in defense of Ah Chan? Should I have told Ah Chan and my father about what was said? These questions were like the darkness he and his father walked through, slowing him down as they made their way to the *milpa*. He'd fallen behind his father and now trotted to catch up, and to leave those questions behind.

As he drew close, Balam smelled the faint smokiness

of the coals his father carried in a clay pot. Today they were going to burn the *milpa*. He hoped that he and his father would break their fast—eat some of the food he carried—before they set the fires. He wanted to be strong, to work like a man, and fasting had sapped his energy.

How did his father do it—not eat and still seem so strong?

H   H   H

The sky was turning pink in the east, when Balam and his father stood in front of a quickly built altar at the edge of the *milpa*. On the ground, in the center of the altar, his father placed the bowl of coals. Into the bowl he shook several chunks of copal—a powdery resin, rich with *itz*, from which black smoke soon began curling, writhing. The smell of copal sneaked into his awareness, subtle and vaguely sweet, as soft to the nose as the feel of an orchid blossom brushing against his cheek.

The copal burned slowly, its plume undulating like a snake climbing the sky. A snake without rattles.

And then his father began praying in a voice that was at once loud but soft, spoken yet full of song.

"Red Chac, lord of the land and the eastern sky, lord of the forest and all things that live: Be patient with us. We are doing as men have always done. We ask for your understanding. Accept our offering of copal. We ask for your forgiveness as we burn your forest so that we may live. Out of this small hurt will come the blood of life.

May no animal of the forest be harmed by our fire."

Uk lifted his face to the sky. "Wind, coming from the east, stained with the blood of Lord Sun's birth, work for us. Where are you Red Wind, wind from the east? Hear my prayer. Bring your strength here, where we have done our work. Breathe life into our fire, our maize, our bodies."

Last year the prayer had been the same, almost word for word. But the power of these words was such that this year Balam heard them as if for the first time. Dropping to his knees, Balam helped his father bury a clay figure, made to resemble one of the four *Bacabob* who hold up the heavens at the four corners. He helped his father bury three more, one at each side of the *milpa*. Thus honored, the *Bacabob* would protect the crops from the dangers of the forest and would also protect the forest from the *milpa's* fire.

As they let their rope sandals soak up water against the fire, Balam and Uk ate the food they had brought. Hungry as he was, Balam found his stomach had grown too small to eat all he craved. The unfamiliar weight of the food caused his gut to cramp. His father looked lost in thoughts. Was his gut cramping also?

"The drought has caused the forest to be almost as dry as the *holche*," Uk said as he tied on a sandal. "When the morning winds come, cinders may be carried far and the line of fire may spread faster than we would like. Be vigilant and don't let anything distract you from stray cinders."

Balam nodded as he tied on the sandals. The sogginess of the rope felt strange against the soles of his feet.

H   H   H

Black smoke billowed, towering above the trees, seeming to rise as high as the clouds of *hahah* should have, clouds that had not yet come. As it stretched across the sky, the smoke softened, looking like clouds before releasing rain. Like clouds, the smoke hid Lord Sun. Unlike clouds, the smoke rained only cinders, and charred or smoldering leaves.

Where were the winds that bring rain? Wind was important for burning *holche*—it made the fire burn hotter and faster and gave it a single direction. Without a strong fire, he and his father might have to burn the *milpa* a second time, which would be much harder with the tinder already turned to ash. Without wind, steady and strong—but not too strong—the burning would take a long time, increasing this time of danger.

Balam chased cinders as he'd once chased butterflies with Tutz, making a game of trying to knock them down from the air. It was as difficult now to hit cinders as to hit butterflies, but unlike butterflies the cinders always fell to the ground, where Balam stomped on them with his water-soaked sandals.

Without wind, the smoke hung motionless in the air, growing thicker. The cinders were becoming more difficult to see. Balam saw his father only as a shadow against the flames. When he looked down at himself, he saw that the smoke's soot and ash had settled on every part of his body. As he worked, sweat slid down his chest and arms and legs, one drop consuming another until the drops were the size and color of slugs, leaving behind slimy trails.

As he worked his skin grew darker, almost black, almost the color the bachelors painted themselves.

His father yelled. "Balam! There!"

Balam raced to where his father pointed, to the western side of the *milpa,* close to the forest's edge.

He squinted. Smoke burned his eyes and seemed to fill his lungs with soot. His chest ached with each breath. As he ran, he hoped the Chacs were watching—the smoke should rouse them, remind them to send the clouds of *hahah*. Ah Chan often said the Chacs saw the smoke of *milpa* fires as a challenge: Whose clouds were greater— those made by men or those made by the Chacs?

Through the smoke he saw a blossom of flame, petals slowly opening, unfolding in a circle. He leaped as high as he could, over the line of fire his father was tending. It was a mighty leap, but not quite high enough—he felt flames lick the insides of his thighs. Once over the flames he was relieved not to be wearing an *ex*—it might have caught fire.

To Balam the flames looked like a flock of grouse, each bird on fire and fleeing a cinder thrown into their midst. His sandals were growing dry. As he stomped on the flames, heat grew more intense on the soles of his feet. As he stomped on the last flame, another fire blossomed next to him.

Balam coughed harder as the smoke thickened. *If only the winds would come!* Balam longed to take refuge upwind from the fire, where smoke would be thinner, where fresh air would chase the blazes. With no winds, the smoke sometimes seemed to pour downward instead of rising.

Tears oozed from Balam's eyes as he glanced up. Where was Lord Sun? How long had they been working? Balam could not tell. The air grew hotter, as if Lord Sun was no longer in the sky but now walked the earth. He saw a cinder streak downward through the blackness. It occurred to him that cinders might be sweat flung off Lord Sun as he strode this way and that. Once a cinder fell directly onto his head, bouncing off, but not before Balam whiffed burning hair.

Balam worked harder than he'd ever worked before, stopping only when he needed to dampen his sandals before they too caught fire. He worked so hard that soon no thoughts other than fighting the fire entered his head. His whole body itched and when he scratched soot peeled off, balling under his fingernails or coming off in long strips.

And then, out of the corner of his eye, he saw a shadow moving in the jerky manner of turtles. Had a turtle, confused by the smoke and noise, decided safety lay in the direction of the fire?

Before he could move to save the turtle, his father called, his voice frantic. "Balam! Here! I need your help!"

Balam ran toward his father, intending to rush back to the turtle before it got much farther. But in the chaos of fighting the fire alongside his father, the turtle lumbered on, out of his thoughts.

Ħ Ħ Ħ

Lord Sun, swollen and red, sank through the smoke, casting his ashen light on the *milpa*. The smell of fire hung in the air and fallen trees smoldered. Balam and his father stood side by side, exhausted, looking at the *milpa*.

"I think it is safe to leave," Uk said.

And then Balam saw the turtle. He pointed, his shaking finger telling his father what words could not. Together they walked to it.

The dead turtle's shell was blackened, but one of its rear legs had not been completely burned—skin, dried and blackened, still clung to bone.

Balam stared for a moment. Uk did not need to tell Balam this was not good. Was this the same turtle he'd seen before, caught by the fire walking in the opposite direction? Had it perhaps been carrying a message for the Chac of rain?

Uk put a hand on Balam's shoulder. "There is no more we can do here. We must go." Where satisfaction should have been, there was now only weariness and doubt.

As they approached the village Balam felt oddly separated from his body, as if he were floating more than walking. And then out of the haze, rushing toward them as if pursued, came Tutz.

He stopped, blocking their way and, staring from Uk to Balam and then back to Uk, he struggled to control his breathing.

"Ix Bacal," he gasped. "Ix Bacal has been taken . . . stolen . . . on the way to the *cenote*! They sent back the two bachelors . . . Cantul and Tuk . . . who were guarding her . . . saying that . . . that each boy must give them part . . . a measure of the seeds of their . . . their blood crop."

All weariness left Balam's body with the cry, "No!"

Together, Balam, Uk, and Tutz ran to the village, to Ah Chan's *palapa*.

Part III
Yellow from the South

Tired as he was, Balam could not sleep. Lying in bed, his body smelled like a smoldering pile of *holche*. Pain flared wherever he moved. His mind seemed to fill with the smoke of these flames, clouding his thoughts of everything but Ix Bacal. Only her face glowed bright as an ember through his discomfort.

He tried to lie still, to dampen the pain, searching in his mind for possible places Ix Bacal might be. Who had taken her? Were they near, waiting to trade her for the seeds of maize?

Seeds! Seeds of maize! What they demanded was now more precious than the seed that sprang from any man's loins. Each generation of maize—the flesh of life, the life of flesh—was as precious as each generation of children. To steal a generation of one meant the death of the other. Like children, maize needed the strength and wisdom of men to be planted and to grow and to be harvested. Maize could not seed itself! Like children, maize could not tend itself! Maize was a gift from the gods in heaven, a link between gods and men! How could the kidnappers demand such a thing? How dare they kidnap Ix Bacal for so outrageous, so repugnant, so impossible a demand?

Such questions were more painful than his muscles from working so hard, more painful than the soles of his feet from cinders that had burned through the rope of his sandals, more painful than his lungs, which lay heavily in his chest, sometimes seeming to flutter and flap like the wings of a wounded bird caught in the cage of his ribs.

In his mind he searched the forest for Ix Bacal. He searched near the rubble of the ancient buildings where the iguanas lived. He searched around his father's *milpa*, looking for movement among the dying leaves of the guava and coral bean bushes. In his mind he searched the ashes of the *milpa* itself, looking for footprints or evidence of struggle. All he saw there was the charred carcass of the turtle.

So strong were these visions that Balam was unaware of falling asleep. As sleep came over him the visions continued, becoming clearer, seeming to take his body with them into the forest as he searched for the girl—the woman—he always expected would become his wife.

H   H   H

Who was the woman walking toward him along the path, her *huipil* so white his eyes ached to look upon it? Balam stopped, ready to flee. Could it be a *xtabai*? She walked so lightly, so quietly that Balam looked to see if her feet touched the ground.

They did not. But Balam, frightened as he was, could not run. When the woman came to within a few steps of him, she stopped. "Balam," she said, smiling. "Do not be afraid." Her voice was at once familiar and strange, half remembered as if in a dream.

Still he could not move, standing as if he were a stalk

of maize with tassels instead of hair, hunched leaves instead of shoulders.

And then he knew who she was. He had never seen his mother. He had never heard her voice. His father had only told him that she had been the most beautiful woman in the world. Ah Chan had said this also, adding that if Balam was lucky he might see the beauty of his mother in the faces of his own daughters.

"Mother?" The heart within his chest seemed to grow, and his voice was more like that of a frog than of a boy.

The woman nodded. "Come. I know where you will find Ix Bacal."

She held out her hand. Her hand was cold but he soon felt the warmth of his own hand reflecting off hers, coming back to him.

"Is she unharmed?" Balam asked. Earlier that evening, the bachelors had spoken of kidnappers forcing themselves on captured women. Balam had tried not to hear, refusing to believe that men would plant their seed where someday his seed should grow.

"Yes, she is well. They are holding her for ransom, that is true. But if the ransom does not bear fruit, they will not violate her. Instead, they will sacrifice her . . . a virgin woman . . . that the gods may bring rain."

"There is time . . . to rescue her?"

"With luck. But even with luck you will need help."

Startled, Balam heard pounding footsteps, growing

louder, coming from behind. He spun around, letting go of his mother's hand, prepared to fight. What demon of the night could be chasing them? If not an *aluxob* or monkey-like *kinkajou*, what marauding enemy might take him hostage to hold with Ix Bacal?

What he saw startled him more than anything he was prepared to fight. Balam found himself looking at a boy he'd never seen before but knew immediately. The boy's face was the one that looked up from the *cenote* when he, Balam, looked down. Balam saw now what had startled him the other day—in the boy's smile lurked unfriendliness, a challenge.

Balam looked down the length of the boy's body. He was naked, but when Balam glanced upward he noticed that the boy had no white bead tied to a strand of his unruly hair. Although he knew who stood before him, Balam was overcome with a defiant sort of shyness.

Looking to his mother, he asked, "My brother?" His voice betrayed both his fear and his excitement. Her nod was interrupted.

"Ask *me*, Balam. Ask *me*. Don't hide behind the *huipil* of our mother."

Balam turned toward the voice that resembled his own, but sounded sharper. "Are you my brother?" he asked, in what he hoped was a manlike voice.

The boy shrugged. "Only if you are mine. Are you? If you are not my brother then you must be a dream." The challenge in his smile deepened, becoming a sneer. "And from such a dream I hope to awaken soon."

"What is your name?" Balam asked through clenched teeth.

"It is not for those who are living to know. Call me Balam Two." He chuckled at his own cleverness. "We have work to do." The boy turned to their mother. "They have moved her . . . toward the *cenote*. We must hurry."

"Go . . . go without me," she said. "I will go at my own pace, in my own way."

Balam felt a hand, cold and hard, grip his. With a tug, his brother pulled him into a trot. "Come *on!*" hissed his brother. "Are you afraid of fighting?"

Balam shook his hand free and sprinted down the trail. He was glad to hear his brother's labored breathing behind him.

"This way!"

Still running, Balam turned to see his brother standing on the trail, pointing into the forest. For the first time since meeting his brother, Balam smiled. The way his brother wished to go was thick with tendrils and jagged chunks of rock pushing up from the ground.

"This way is easier . . . quicker," Balam said, nodding smugly over his left shoulder toward a game trail that wound through the forest, made perhaps by peccaries or deer or even jaguars.

"Only if you are human." Stubbornness narrowed his brother's eyes and pushed out his lower lip. In spite of himself, Balam laughed. It was amusing to see in his brother what he, himself, must look like when he was vexed.

"Go that way if you wish," Balam said. "We will see who gets to the *cenote* first."

Balam turned and trotted to where the game trail veered off the main trail. He expected to hear his brother's footsteps follow. He heard nothing and grinned. How could someone from the other world think he knew this forest better than one who lived here?

Balam heard voices from the direction of the *cenote*. They grew louder as he approached, carefully, quietly. One voice rose above the others, saying, "We cannot wait. The forest is thick with men from the village. Unbind her hands and feet so that she may walk into the water."

Creeping closer, Balam peered through the undergrowth and saw a cluster of men, their bodies painted black, standing around Ix Bacal. One was untying a rope that bound her hands. Balam was proud of the way she held her head high, not looking at her captors.

What could he do? He saw four men with spears. Even if his brother finally found his way to the *cenote*, what could two boys do against that many men? Nothing came to mind, even as the man began untying the rope that bound Ix Bacal's feet.

He had to do something. Even if it cost him his life, Balam knew he must try to set Ix Bacal free. He would be unable to live knowing that he had hidden in the forest, watching as she dropped into the *cenote*.

Just as he was about to rise up, shouting, a cry came from beyond the men, from the forest. It raised the hair on the back of his neck and caused him to catch his breath. There was only one thing it could be: an angry jaguar, ready to attack.

All the men turned toward the sound, their weapons ready but trembling in their hands. As they took several steps toward the sound, Balam stumbled into the clearing and rushed toward Ix Bacal. Running, he grabbed one of her hands. Her startled eyes softened as she realized who he was. Her feet were still tied and, unable to run, she toppled into Balam's arms. Would his luck hold? Grunting, he began dragging her toward the forest when one of the men looked back and saw what he was doing.

The man ran toward Balam and Ix Bacal, just as another shriek came from the forest—louder this time and more angry than before. The man hesitated, fear causing him to crouch as he ran, but he didn't stop. He wrenched Ix Bacal from Balam's arms and, lifting her to his shoulders, staggered back to the *cenote*.

"No!" Balam cried.

The other men turned toward his cry.

"Accept our gift, Lords of Xibalba!" bellowed the man who now held Ix Bacal over the *cenote's* edge. "Don't torment the Chacs . . . do not fight . . . allow the rains to come that we may give you more!" He threw his arms wide. Ix Bacal disappeared over the side of the *cenote*.

"No!" Balam shrieked again, his voice burning his throat like lightning, echoing in the forest like thunder.

And then the cry of the jaguar came again, turning all heads. From the forest stepped a horrible beast: Not man or jaguar, but the most fierce combination of both, staggering on its hind legs, like those of a man but twisted into the shape of a jaguar's. The eyes of the beast glowed yellow and the sound of its voice seemed to issue like smoke from its mouth.

Onward it staggered, raking the air with its claws. The men cried, running past Balam, smelling of fear, whimpering.

As he watched the specter approach, Balam was too frightened, too distraught, to move. The were-jaguar was between him and Ix Bacal. What could he do? Suddenly, the beast drew himself up and its skin sluffed off as if flayed, falling about its feet in a heap. Where a monster had stood now stood Balam's brother.

"Quick!" Balam's brother grabbed the *cenote's* rope and ran to Balam. As he spoke, he tied the rope around Balam's waist. "Jump in after her and I will pull you up."

Balam stared for a moment at his brother. Could he trust him?

There was nothing else he could do.

Balam tripped running to the *cenote* and scrambled to its edge, plunging headfirst into the water. Down, down, down he fell until the rope jerked at his middle, burning his skin as it pulled tight. He grabbed the rope with his hands and pulled up, looking through water as if through tears. Up and up he went until his face burst from water, into air.

Gasping, he felt Ix Bacal next to him, floating. He grabbed for her, but at his touch she sank, just out of reach, motionless. Balam thrashed at the water, trying to draw himself closer but down she sank, as if pulled from below, just as he felt himself pulled from the water.

"She is dead, Balam!" His brother called from above. "Let her go. Let her go. It is not so bad to be dead. I should know!"

And then, as if from the *cenote's* depths, from Xibalba itself, came a cry of sorrow, of rage, of disbelief. Balam thrashed in the air, struggling to go down as he was pulled up, bellowing with anger and fear and sorrow.

Rock scraped his skin as his brother pulled him over a lip of rock and onto the ground.

Sobbing, Balam retched water even as he tried to crawl back to the *cenote's* edge. And then he felt a hand stroke his shoulder and back. "Your brother is right, Balam," came his mother's voice. "Ix Bacal is with us now. We will take good care of her."

Balam fumbled for the hand that stroked him. "Mother! Mother!" he cried. "Mother!" He felt himself lifted and cradled. His sobs began to calm and he felt himself relaxing, as if falling asleep. But he did not want to sleep! Not now!

Struggling to open his eyes, he looked through tears,

his lungs heavy, as if filled with water. Balam was startled to see the gentle face of Nakin.

Suddenly, Balam had never been more awake. She hummed to him as she often had when he was small and scared or hurt. She hummed and stroked the top of his head and his forehead and his chest.

Catching her breath she pulled away her hand. "What happened, Balam?" she asked, reaching toward his chest again.

Looking toward the smell of smoldering *holche,* toward the pain that burned on his stomach and chest, he saw a scrape—made by rock against the skin of his belly—and the angry stripe around his middle from where a rope had burned against his skin.

NINE

"How is the dog?" Ah Chan asked. "Growing fat?"

Balam nodded. "As fat as Tooch grows skinny."

"Someday he will understand the need of what we do." The old man studied Balam. "You grow skinny also. Are you fasting?"

It was a question Balam had dreaded. Rain had yet to fall and the men and bachelors in the village had been fasting for two days, cleansing themselves for the three-day *Ch'achac* ceremony. Although he had told nobody, Balam had been fasting too, adding his food to what he fed the dog. It was true that he wished to prepare himself for the *Ch'achac* as a man would. But it was more true that he simply had no appetite since Ix Bacal had been taken.

Reluctantly, he nodded, lowering his eyes, expecting Ah Chan to scold, telling him it was not right for a boy to fast.

Instead, Ah Chan said, "We all mourn for Ix Bacal."

To Balam's relief his voice was gentle. "She may yet be found."

Balam nodded, even though through dreaming he'd been transported to where Ix Bacal had perished in a *cenote,* most likely their own. Believing this, having witnessed this, made swallowing water fetched from the *cenote* difficult for Balam.

"It is good you have fasted," Ah Chan continued. "I need the help of someone pure in mind and body, and you are the one whose help I want."

Ah Chan wanted him to help prepare for the *Ch'achac*? Wasn't that usually a job for one of his four helpers, the village elders, or for one of the bachelors?

"I am pleased to help," he said, trying to smile.

"Good." Ah Chan leaned forward. "Of all the boys in the village, you hold the most promise of. . . ." He straightened his back. "After you feed the dog, come to my *palapa.* I'll be waiting."

H   H   H

The dog was always grateful for the food Balam brought. Instead of scavenging or relying on stolen scraps from Tooch, it now ate what the family ate. Grateful as it was for food, Balam sensed it was most grateful for his attention. Before, Balam had either ignored the dog or treated it rudely, trying to discourage it from becoming a pet of his brother's. It had always shied from him. Now, as Balam approached, its whole body wagged with happiness.

"Leave us alone," Tooch growled, grabbing what Balam brought so he could feed the dog.

Balam watched as the dog tore at the food, hardly chewing before swallowing. There was no reason for Tooch to be jealous. Balam pitied the dog—the way it ate with an eye on him, as if it were afraid Balam might change his mind and take the food away—the way it groveled in happiness, unable to bark—the way it rolled onto its back, so excited it sometimes leaked urine onto its own belly.

Now that the dog was tied to a stake beyond the cooking shed, Tooch never left its side. For the past two nights he'd slept there, willing to risk the pranks of forest spirits to be with the dog, trusting the dog to protect him when in fact the dog looked to Tooch for protection.

Balam tried once more to help his brother understand the importance of sacrificing the dog. "You know why we do this?"

This was a question that answered itself in the asking. Tooch turned away from Balam, refusing to acknowledge it.

"We must give to the gods the best we have. You should be proud to give this dog to the gods. To do so will help us all." Another thought entered Balam's head. "If the dog knew how much he will help us . . . you especially . . . he would gladly allow himself to be sacrificed. If you were attacked by a peccary, wouldn't he come to your aid, risking his life to save yours?"

Tooch didn't respond. Perhaps he didn't understand, in spite of the clear way in which Balam had explained all of this. Or perhaps Tooch, in spite of what he wanted to believe, knew the dog would most likely run scared if a peccary so much as looked in its direction.

"Tooch, without rain we will die. Giving the dog's flesh and blood . . . his *ch'ulel* . . . to the gods will help bring *hahah*." Balam suddenly felt tired of trying to reason with his brother. It was so simple. How could something so simple be so difficult for Tooch to accept? Was he really as simple as some people said?

Tooch hunched forward, touching his forehead to his drawn-up knees. "Leave us alone," he said. The dog finished the last morsel and walked to Tooch, nosing him.

Before leaving, Balam watched the dog sniff the boy's neck and under his knees. Was the dog looking for more food? For affection? Perhaps both held the same meaning for dogs—and for people—and for the thirteen gods in heaven.

H   H   H

As always, it was difficult to keep up with Ah Chan— the old man's legs were long and he never seemed to tire. Balam found it more difficult still, clasping to his chest a large clay pot. They were not following a trail, but Ah Chan seemed to know every obstacle. After stumbling several times, Balam decided not to watch for obstacles himself, but to mimic—to step high where Ah Chan stepped high, to veer where Ah Chan veered. The more he trusted Ah Chan's judgment, the less he stumbled.

At first they walked quietly, not speaking. Not once did Ah Chan look back to see if Balam was able to keep up. Even so, the old man slowed when Balam lagged and sped up when Balam drew close.

Where were they going? Balam wasn't even sure in which direction they were headed. East, perhaps? Or a little north?

And were they safe, this far from the village?

"There are no men lurking in this part of the forest," Ah Chan said, as if Balam had asked this last question aloud. "They have gone back to their village, to protect their families from the revenge they think our men will surely seek."

"What village did they come from?" Balam asked. He found Ah Chan's voice reassuring and he didn't want to let Ah Chan's words disappear like bats into the unfamiliar shadows of the forest.

"I have heard they came from Tzebtun. Of that I cannot be certain, but it is possible. Last year the men there planted maize according to the calendar, not the weather or the stars. They did not wait until the rains came daily . . . until *hahah.*"

Balam dodged a branch that sprung back from Ah Chan, almost hitting him in the face. When the men go to Tzebtun for revenge, he thought, I want to be with them.

"Did you foresee that last year it would rain only

once?" This was a question he'd been afraid to ask his godfather for a long time. But struggling to keep up with Ah Chan, dodging this way and that, seemed to have flushed this question from the safe place in which it had been hiding.

Balam was relieved to hear Ah Chan chuckle. "No one else has been brave enough to ask me that question. I tell you honestly: I did not know for certain, but I suspected the rains might not come. We live in an unsettled time . . . a time in which we have lost much of the power we once had to communicate with our gods. We have scattered from our temples . . . from Chichén Itzá. And it seems our gods are distracted, too . . . perhaps fighting among themselves, dissatisfied and bored . . . perhaps sick. And," he said, "it has been a long time since we sacrificed one of our own, for the benefit of all . . . the gods and man."

Balam was listening so carefully he stumbled, almost falling on the pot he carried. "Did you see these things in the stars . . . or the dice?"

"Both," came the old man's reply. "And I saw things in our hearts as well. We have grown stingy. We have forgotten how much our gods depend on us for nourishment, just as we depend on them for rain. We have been distracted also by invaders from the north, and by feuds among our scattered villages."

"The bachelors say we do not have an *ahman* powerful enough to communicate . . ." Balam stopped, realizing too late what an insult this was to Ah Chan. Had he been too long among the bachelors—speaking whatever came to his mind regardless of how proper or insulting or repugnant it was?

Ah Chan walked on. Was it possible that he hadn't heard the question? "*Wac,*" the old man cursed, as he walked into a branch. "Do you think what the bachelors say is true?"

"No," Balam replied. But Balam had been impressed that the bachelors were brave enough to think such a thought and dared say it aloud.

"It is kind of you to defend me, but there is some truth to what they say. Some things are too great for any man to know. And some things must be endured. I cannot cause Venus to alter his path across the sky. I do not know how well the gods of the thirteen heavens wage war on the seven gods of Xibalba. I do not stand atop a great pyramid where the Chacs cannot ignore me. I simply do what I can. Sometimes that is not enough."

They continued walking in silence. When Ah Chan stopped, Balam looked around, puzzled, wondering why.

"Do you notice anything unusual?" Ah Chan asked.

Balam looked about some more. What was he not seeing? He shook his head.

"Good." Ah Chan sounded pleased.

Balam continued looking. He peered behind himself. Seeing nothing, he turned back to ask Ah Chan what he was missing. Ah Chan had vanished.

Balam began to tremble. Were *xtabai* playing pranks on them? He glanced nervously around, expecting men from Tzebtun to pounce on him next. Should he run? He didn't know where he was or where his village lay. Should he shout?

His throat was tight—only a strangled noise came out. And then, as if from far away, he heard Ah Chan's voice.

"Balam?"

From which direction was the old man's voice coming? Balam looked to where Ah Chan had been standing. Could the ground have swallowed him up?

"I am here." The voice was clear. Startled, Balam saw Ah Chan's head near the ground, looking at him from behind a huge ceiba tree. "Come," he said.

Balam walked cautiously, not trusting the ground. As he rounded the trunk of the tree, he saw Ah Chan standing between two massive roots forming a crude arch over a dark, burrow-like hole. Ah Chan held in his hand a small sopadilla branch. "Gather some sticks for making a fire," he said.

The branch made more smoke than light, but Balam was grateful for what little light it made. The tunnel was low. Balam hunched to avoid hitting his head. He saw only the moving darkness of Ah Chan ahead and marveled at the way in which the old man fit his great height into the tunnel. Down they went, first one way and then another, seeming almost to circle back on themselves.

The pulsing shadows and smoke made the old man appear to dance more than walk. He did not know how close he was to Ah Chan until he bumped into him.

With surprise, Balam saw Ah Chan was standing. They were in a small cavern, large enough only for several men. The sound of their breathing was as loud as snoring, and Balam felt for a moment as if he'd walked into the mouth of a giant, sleeping jaguar. Tooth-like rocks hung from the cave's ceiling, dripping into pots a liquid Balam imagined might be saliva. The moist air was almost like breath—taking on the odor of their two bodies, just as the breath of a jaguar must take on the odor of its caught prey.

"Never tell where you have been." Ah Chan's voice was strangely subdued. "This is where we collect *zuhuy ha*, virgin water . . . water that has never been touched by the hands of women or men."

Peering into the flickering shadows, Balam noticed many small clay statues to the Chacs on shelves carved into the cave's wall. And near the pots that collected water were smaller vessels, partly filled with the ash of incense. Surrounding the pots, Balam noticed piles of shards where pots must have been dropped in the dim light and the bad air that even now made Balam dizzy.

From a fold of his *ex* Ah Chan drew a clay figure. "Place this with the others," he said, taking the pot from Balam's arms. The shards crunched underfoot as he made his way to the shelves.

This done, Ah Chan lifted each clay pot, pouring water into the pot they had brought. When they left the cave, the way out seemed much shorter than the way in.

H   H   H

Balam drew himself up, sitting, when he heard his father stir. It was still dark. He had tried to sleep, but the distant sound of Ah Chan's voice, coming from the altar in the plaza, had startled him into wakefulness whenever sleep seemed ready to take him. For two days, Ah Chan had been praying while the altar was built, while everything was made ready for the *Ch'achac*.

Together, Balam and his father walked silently from the *palapa* to the plaza. In the dark Balam saw the shapes of men standing a respectful distance from the altar under the branches of the ceiba tree. Still, he and his father were among the first to gather.

Ah Chan was now silent, standing in front of the altar, his head bowed, as darkness seemed to seep into the ground, disappearing like rain into soil. He was flanked by the village's four elders, Ah Chan's helpers. Just as Lord Sun's light burst over the tops of the trees, Ah Chan lifted his face. The old man's face flashed crimson, as if splashed by blood. As the color ran from his face, he lifted his arms and began to chant in a voice that made it difficult for Balam to understand many of the words. Balam hoped the Chac gods understood.

Circling the altar Ah Chan prayed and chanted. Occasionally a shadow scurried from the growing crowd to place an offering of food or copal on the platform between its four upright poles. In his hands, Ah Chan held a shallow bowl filled with coals and as he passed by the four elders, one now stationed at each corner of the altar, they sprinkled copal into the coals. Sweet smoke billowed each time from the bowl in his hands.

Often Ah Chan would reach with his voice, taking it higher. In that way he showed respect for the Chacs to whom he spoke. The four men began hitting chopping sticks together, making the sound of lightning, and soon two of them dropped their sticks. These two began pounding on turtle drums, making the sound of thunder.

Clouds of incense and the sounds of lightning and thunder filled the plaza. Surely the Chacs would notice.

Sweat glistened on the great expanse of Ah Chan's forehead. He had not slept for two days, had never dozed, yet he seemed to grow stronger with each circle around the altar.

At intervals Ah Chan lowered his head. He would then squat, reaching under the altar, taking out a calabash of the virgin water he and Balam had fetched. He would pour water into the bowls each of the four elders held toward him. They would walk to the four directions of the plaza, offering water to the Chacs, sprinkling the people who had gathered.

Several times Ah Chan did not retrieve virgin water. Instead, when he squatted he took out a calabash of *balche*. After pouring some into bowls the four men walked around the circle of people, offering sips to everyone. It was bitter, this liquor made of virgin water and honey and bark from the balché tree. For the first few sips, the *balche's* fumes rose through the back of Balam's nose to his eyes, stinging, bringing tears. After a while the liquor seemed hardly to go to his stomach. Instead, it went from his mouth to his head, making him at once happy and sad, sleepy and awake. By then the *balche* had lost its bitterness and his tongue had lost much of its feeling.

Suddenly six excited, noisy turkeys appeared, seemingly from nowhere. The four elders held each turkey, two by its wings and two by its legs, as Ah Chan poured *balche* down its protesting throat nine times. The birds, becoming drunker with each sip, were soon docile. They did not seem to mind dying as their blood spilled into bowls to be burned, their *ch'ulel* offered to the Chacs as smoke.

A little while later, Ah Chan cried out: "Who will honor us with the sounds of the frog?"

From the fringes of the plaza came a scurrying. The boys of the village crowded around Ah Chan, pushing each other to be closer. Balam fought an urge to join the boys he'd led not long ago. As he looked they seemed to him so small and childish now. He did not feel part of them anymore.

Balam was pleased to see Tooch standing off to the side of the jostling boys, pleased to see his brother had left his dog to be part of this ceremony. Perhaps Tooch was coming to his senses. Ah Chan pointed first to one boy and then another and another. The last he pointed to was Tooch. Each of the four elders took a boy to the altar, tying him by a leg to a pole, and then standing guard.

Balam knew well what the boys were to do—he had performed this twice before when he was younger. He watched as Tooch crouched, sitting like a frog, as did the other boys. As the four elders beat on turtle shells and hit chopping sticks together, the boys began making the sounds of frogs.

"Woh, woh! Woh, woh! Woh, woh!"

Balam smiled. Tooch sounded just like a frog. And just like a frog, his younger brother lowered his bottom with each sound.

Around the altar went Ah Chan, his voice reaching higher. The frogs kept up their call as the drums beat and the sticks clashed.

On Ah Chan's command, each frog began to cry louder and the drums beat faster. *"Woh, woh! Woh, woh!"* They grew red in the face as they strained. Balam knew what was about to happen when Tooch's eyes grew large. *"Woh, woh! Woh, woh!"* One by one, and still crouching, each boy began to urinate. Urine splashed against the dirt under each boy, splashing mud against their calves and thighs and bellies.

One by one the boys grew silent as they finished.

Only Tooch's stream continued—and continued. Laughter broke out among the crowd that had gathered as Tooch continued to call, his solitary frog voice sounding suddenly thin. Balam could tell his brother was trying not to look proud as mud continued splashing and his rear end continued bobbing. At last he too was silent.

A cheer went up from the crowd and Ah Chan raised his hands, facing the people of the village. The drums now beat a dancing rhythm and people lifted their heels and their voices in happiness for such a fine ending of the *Ch'achac*.

Surely, Balam thought, rain would come soon.

TEN

The great ceiba tree continued to grow weak. Since the *Ch'achac* two days before, Balam had taken it upon himself each morning to pick up the leaves and branches that fell from it during the night.

At first he didn't know what compelled him to do this. But when he finished and looked at the cleared area under the tree, its shadow looking like water soaking into dirt, he knew why. Since he was fasting again, it was one way to keep his mind off an empty stomach. But more important, with the ground cleared he could once again hope rain was coming. Such hope was impossible with leaves and branches on the ground to remind him of drought.

He was not alone in hoping. This morning, on his way to the plaza, Balam had seen several men on the roofs of their *palapas,* tightening thatch against rain. Nakin had been going through the seed maize, picking out rotten kernels. On his way to the plaza, Balam saw other women in their courtyards doing the same.

This morning, as he worked under the ceiba, he often stole glances at the sky showing through gaps in the tree's foliage. He saw no clouds. Each day Lord Sun seemed brighter and hotter. Was it possible Lord Sun had grown too strong?

"Balam."

Leaves and twigs in his hand, Balam stood and looked toward Ah Chan. The old man seemed more tired now than after three days of not sleeping during the *Ch'achac*. "Yes?"

"It is time to fetch the dog."

Balam nodded. He had known since yesterday that Ah Chan was preparing for the dog's sacrifice. What else could be done as the drought continued, especially after the *Ch'achac*? Even if rain had come, the dog would have been sacrificed in thanks.

"Tell Tooch how honored we are to offer this dog's *ch'ulel* to the gods."

Once more Balam nodded. He was not eager to face Tooch. But surely someday Tooch would understand, and be proud.

As Balam walked toward his family's *palapa*, he searched the sky. Were clouds gathering just beyond sight, behind the tops of the trees? It seemed the longer the rains waited, the more Balam—and others—smelled or heard signs of rain. Just yesterday a girl had come running to Ah

Chan, saying she heard the croaking of tree frogs in the forest. Such a sure sign of rain had caused Ah Chan's somber face to light up. He had picked up the girl and run. Balam had hurried behind, wanting to be among the first to see this wonderful thing. Before long, it seemed half the village ran to keep up with the old man.

"Over there! Over there!" the girl had cried. And, sure enough, Balam heard it too: several loud, long croaks. "Here! Here!" Ah Chan had put the girl down and everyone had scattered, looking for frogs.

Balam had stayed close to Ah Chan, who listened and looked up into a sopadilla tree. Balam followed the old man's gaze. There, on a branch, was perched a toucan. As they looked it flew to a higher branch, squawking, looking down defiantly. And then it had opened its mouth and croaked—sounding just like a frog. It was a sound toucans sometimes made.

Excitedly, everyone from the village gathered around Ah Chan, growing puzzled that he was looking at a bird. And then suddenly they knew. One of the men picked up a rock to throw when Ah Chan lifted his hand. "The bird is not to blame. Let it be."

Reluctantly, everyone had gone back to the village. Only Balam had lingered, hoping perhaps the toucan had been inspired to imitate croaking tree frogs and then had been scared into silence by the commotion of people. When the toucan flew off, it took with it the sound of tree frogs.

As Balam walked toward his *palapa,* he tried not to hear the sound of rain in the forest leaves, so dry now that the slightest breeze made them rustle loudly, the way lush, healthy leaves would have sounded in a downpour. He nodded a greeting toward his mother and brother as he walked through the courtyard. Skirting the main *palapa,* he walked by the cooking shed. His *chichi* looked up.

"It is time?"

Balam nodded.

"Send Tooch to me. Tell him I need help. Or tell him I have a treat. That should make your work easier." She looked down at the breadnut she was cutting into pieces.

"Thank you, *Chichi.*" As he looked at her sagging skin and wrinkled face he regretted the times he'd compared her to an overripe papaya. When he was younger, after kindness such as she'd just shown, he would have thrown his arms around her. He longed to do that now but resisted this childish impulse, instead continuing toward the place where the dog was tied.

He looked for Tooch as he approached. He didn't see his brother where he expected to. Was this good luck or bad? Had his brother chosen this moment to go off into the forest to relieve himself? Or to play? Balam began to hurry, to take advantage of this luck until it occurred to him that the boy might be waiting to ambush him.

Wary now, stepping closer, he saw that the dog was missing too.

"*Wac!*" Balam cursed. Where the dog had been was now only trampled, bare ground. The rope was gone from where it had been tied.

What does the little monkey think he's doing? How did he know this was the time? Balam fisted his hands in anger. Did his brother truly think the dog was more important than the welfare of the entire village? What would Ah Chan say? What would their father say?

And then a horrible thought struck. Was it possible Tooch and the dog had been captured by men from another village? Yesterday, one of the bachelors claimed he saw evidence of strangers lurking in the forest. Most of the men thought it was a story invented to gather support for raids the bachelors had been planning since Ix Bacal disappeared. But what if the bachelor truly had seen a stranger?

What should he do? Balam didn't want to look foolish to the men in the village, voicing a fear that proved to be groundless. But without such a fear he would go back to Ah Chan's *palapa* empty-handed, looking equally foolish.

Balam felt the sting of tears. Tooch was not only embarrassing himself, but his family—he was embarrassing the entire village in the eyes of the gods.

When Balam heard screaming, as if from a swooping bird, he felt at once furious and relieved. Tooch stumbled toward him, his face red and streaked with tears. He was sobbing so hard he could barely breathe.

"Ba-Ba-Balam!" He stood in front of Balam, his shoulders shaking, struggling to speak. "The dog . . . in the *milpa*. Come!"

His brother turned, running back the way he'd come. Balam followed, surprised to find himself struggling to keep up. The emptiness of his stomach seemed to have risen to his head.

Out of the forest he ran. Tooch was already halfway across the *milpa,* puffs of ash rising from where his feet struck. He was headed toward the opposite edge of the *milpa,* toward the small altar he and his father had built after the burning. As he ran Balam saw his brother slide to a stop. A scream filled the clearing, so loud Balam could hardly believe it came from his brother. Balam ran up and looked to where Tooch was staring.

For a moment he felt what Tooch must be feeling. In front of the altar lay the dog, its head and neck swollen to enormous size. Above where the rope encircled its neck, its skin was stretched taut and Balam saw its hind legs twitch. No eyes stared—they were lost in tautly swollen skin. Even the ears were lost. Blood oozed from where eyes and ears should be.

Balam gasped. Trapped under the weight of the dog's head was the bloodied, chewed length of a rattlesnake, still struggling to move, even in death. The snake's tail was a partially healed stump with no rattles.

As they stared, the dog's legs stopped twitching and its chest grew still.

H   H   H

The beat of turtle drums seemed to grow louder as darkness drew itself more tightly around those gathered under the great ceiba tree. People crowded forward. Were they pushed by darkness or trying to protect the fire from darkness? Smoke from the fire undulated like lianas dangling upward instead of down.

Ah Chan threw lumps of copal into the fire—thirteen in all—one for each heaven. Balam watched the flames chase shadows back and forth across the old man's face. Even the flames seemed to dance to the rhythm of the drums and his heart obeyed also—pounding against his chest as if his chest were a turtle shell.

The Chacs would have to be deaf not to hear, blind not to be impressed. Who in heaven would be unable to smell so much copal smoke becoming one with the darkness?

After the last of the copal went into the fire, Ah Chan beckoned a young woman, not yet wed, to step forward from the crowd. She knelt before him and bowed her head. Using an awl made from the bone of a long-dead ancestor, Ah Chan pierced her ears, slowly drawing a length of rope through each hole.

The soaked rope he offered to the Chacs, dropping it into the fire, where it hissed like angry snakes, its dark smoke slithering upward. Ah Chan stared at the smoke as it rose, with eyes that seemed to see in the smoke apparitions those around him could not see.

Several women and men came forward to have their

ears pierced. Each time, a bowl of *balche* was passed around the ceiba tree. Each person, including Balam, took a sip.

From the crowd stepped the bachelor, Cuc. He took the bone awl from Ah Chan and pierced the fleshy part of his own upper arms. Blood flowed freely, pumping out to the beat of the turtle drums. Quickly, he stepped to the fire, holding out his arms, letting the blood fall directly onto the flames.

Several young men followed Cuc's example. The smell of burning blood filled the plaza.

Next, Ix Bacal's mother stepped forward. The pain of losing her daughter seemed baked onto her hardened face. She knelt before Ah Chan. Instead of bowing her head, she looked up, opened her mouth, and presented her tongue. Two of the four elders helped hold her head in place as Ah Chan pierced the middle of her tongue with a swift downward jab. The elders held her upright as she grew faint with pain. Another elder came forward with a bowl, which he held under her chin, catching the blood that flowed as Ah Chan drew a length of rope through the wound. The old man threw the bloodied rope into the fire, where the shadows made it seem to writhe as though alive.

For a moment she gagged on blood flowing so fast she could not help swallowing some.

More women stepped forward, raising their faces and letting Ah Chan pierce their tongues with the awl. So much blood was poured onto the fire it began to die. Balam and several boys fetched wood from a pile that lay just beyond the fire's light.

The beating of the drums continued, never seeming to grow tired. The men who beat the drums looked dazed, as if in trances. Many other faces, illuminated by the fire, looked dazed from too much *balche,* pain, and loss of blood.

After the last tongue was pierced, Ah Chan raised his hand to the drummers. Silence came so suddenly Balam felt as if his own heart had made a fist of itself.

"Never have we given so much blood at one time to the gods," Ah Chan announced. "But we must do more."

The old man looked around the circle of faces, many of them streaked with blood that seeped from the corners of tightly closed mouths or dripped from ears or arms. His eyes came to rest on Balam.

"Come forward, Balam, and collect my blood."

Dizzy with *balche* and drums and smoke, Balam stepped toward Ah Chan. The ground itself seemed to sway as he walked, and the hand of one of the elders reached out to steady him. Another hand placed the bowl used to gather blood in his hands.

A hand urged Balam to kneel in front of Ah Chan. Ah Chan grasped the boy's shoulder for balance as he, too, knelt. Standing behind him and to the sides were the four elders, blocking Ah Chan from view.

"From our loins come life!" Ah Chan called in a voice

that reached high. "We return to you the *ch'ulel* that you have given!"

Balam tried to avert his gaze. He could not keep from watching as the old man lifted the front of his *ex* and drew out his penis. It was gnarled and thick as a piece of coral vine. Holding his penis as if it were an ear of maize to be de-husked, Ah Chan plunged the awl into the tip, through foreskin. But instead of peeling back the foreskin as if it were husk, he pulled the awl through.

A stream of blood ran over the tip of his penis, steady as urine, into the bowl Balam held. As the stream became a trickle Ah Chan drew a very long, very thick piece of rope partway through the wound before lowering the flap of his *ex* to its proper place. A spot of red grew on the white cloth. The old man's hands were slick with his own blood.

The four elders stepped back as Ah Chan once more used Balam's shoulder to push himself up onto his feet. Hands, seemingly from nowhere, lifted Balam upward and turned him around, toward the fire.

"Who else will give of their blood, that the gods may grow strong?" Ah Chan shouted.

One by one, men came forward and knelt. For each one, Balam held the bowl. The ground continued to sway, as if the earth was carried on the back of a turtle that was drunk as Balam. As he watched, each penis began to look more and more like a dried ear of maize to be husked—held at the waist, pierced with an awl, shucked. But maize does not bleed! Balam scolded himself as he watched blood flow into the bowl in his hands.

One by one, through their wounds, each man drew a length of the same rope that was still connected to Ah Chan, stringing each one to the others. The bowl filled with blood many times. Many times it was taken from Balam's hands to be poured into the fire.

When no more men came forward, they stood in unison. Their *ex* were stained, as if with the blood of birth. And their faces showed the strain of bloodletting and pain. One by one, beginning with Ah Chan, they drew the rope completely through.

"May our blood make you strong," Ah Chan's voice called to the gods. All of those gathered cheered Ah Chan's words and the calabashes of *balche* that suddenly appeared.

Ah Chan stood in a trance, staring at the fire. Once more the old man's face looked drained of life and his eyes seemed to look beyond the flames. Was he traveling again, visiting the heavens or Xibalba? When Ah Chan began to speak, the words made no sense—coming out faster and faster. The old man leapt to one side, shouting, and began to dance and to dodge. Frightened, Balam stepped into the shadows of the ceiba tree.

A voice came from the darkness behind. "You are afraid to use this?"

Balam turned and saw Cuc, who held in his hands an awl. Behind Cuc stood several bachelors, including Tutz.

Blood still dripped from their earlobes or their arms.

"No," Balam replied.

"I don't believe you," said Cuc.

As if in a dream, Balam raised the spine to one ear. His hand shook. Tutz stepped forward. "Let me guide your hand," he said quietly. Balam tried to smile in gratitude, but his mouth would not move. Holding his breath, Balam jabbed.

The shock of pain came a moment after he pulled the awl through. His thoughts became large and bright as the sun—like all the stars gathered together.

"The other ear," Tutz encouraged, guiding Balam's hand again. Once more he tensed with pain, at the same time feeling relieved for pain on both sides of his head, equal and balanced. Blood dripped onto his shoulders, trickling down his back.

He stared at Cuc with defiance and hatred. Was he satisfied?

Just then all heads turned to the approaching sound of wailing. The dancing stopped and the drumbeats ceased. Balam saw Nakin rush to Ah Chan, followed by his *chichi*.

"The seeds!" she cried. "The seeds I sorted are gone! Stolen! Stolen while we were here!"

"Stolen!" his *chichi* echoed.

The stunned silence was shattered by angry shouts as people scattered, rushing to their own *palapa*s. When Balam turned back to where the bachelors had stood, he saw that they, too, were gone.

Balam walked to where Nakin had collapsed. Ah Chan knelt, trying to comfort her. Uk held *Chichi,* who was sobbing. Balam had never seen her cry before. Tooch stood off to the side, silent and grim. He had refused to speak since the death of the mute dog.

Balam walked up to him and tried to put an arm around his shoulders. He wanted to comfort his brother, to draw him close. Tooch shrugged him off, pushing at him. His arm hit the awl in Balam's hand. Clutching his wound, looking at Balam as if he'd been struck in anger, Tooch turned and walked back to their *palapa,* too angry or sad or both to be afraid of what might be lurking in the darkness.

ELEVEN

From near the top of the giant ceiba tree the village seemed unusually quiet. Balam could hear no sounds other than leaves rustling. Where were birds? Where was the macaw his brother had almost caught? Without birds, the tree seemed even closer to death. Wasn't it through birds that trees sang?

The unusual quiet made Balam uneasy. Even so, it was wonderful to command such a view. Was it like this on top of the great pyramids at Chichén Itzá that Ah Chan sometimes described? Being able to see over the top of the forest was wonderful, even though Balam knew it was possible only because the ceiba tree was dying. If the tree were healthy, its thick foliage would block the view. From the branch he straddled, Balam could see almost every *palapa* in the village. What he could not see were clouds.

Gazing down at Ah Chan's *palapa*, Balam was

amazed he'd never climbed this tree before now. He remembered having thought about it several times when he was younger, but he'd been too small then, and scared—it was a sacred tree, after all, and climbing it had seemed somehow wrong. Even now, as large as he was, reaching the first branch had been as tricky as deciding to climb the tree in the first place. Ceiba trees did not grow in ways that made climbing easy.

He wondered now if he'd wished to do other things when he was younger, things that were too difficult then, things he'd forgotten but might now be able to do. One thing he'd never wished to do when he was younger was curse the gods in heaven. Today, sitting in the ceiba, he wanted to hurl profanity at them, to berate all of them for their cruelty and neglect.

What would become of the village in the absence of rain? What would become of his family now that they had no seed left for the next crop of maize?

Even if they came soon, rains would not be able to wash away the village's anger and pain. Not every *pala-pa* had been raided. But several other families had no maize for sowing. No, rain would not help Balam and his family—it would only fall on their *milpa*, barren of seed—it would only wash away the thin soil—and their hopes with it.

Hatred burned in Balam's heart. Perhaps now the bachelors' plans for revenge would be carried out. Perhaps now the men in the village would listen with respect instead of treating the bachelors like young boys at play.

Balam was growing uncomfortable sitting in the tree. Looking about to see if anyone would notice, he prepared to come down when Ah Chan stepped from his *palapa* and squatted outside his door. Balam shrank back, pressing himself against the trunk, not wanting Ah Chan to see him.

"*Wac,*" he cursed under his breath, silently scolding himself for being a careless little boy in a body almost that of a man's. What if it was wrong to climb the sacred ceiba? Would it further provoke the gods?

Balam tensed, hoping Ah Chan would not see him. Luckily, the old man didn't look at the tree, instead seeming lost in thoughts, once more drained of life, as if traveling to other worlds. Balam knew he would have to be patient. He tried to make himself more comfortable, but soon his legs began to cramp and his bottom grew numb. The tree's bark dug into his back.

What could Ah Chan be thinking about? The drought? The dog? The blind fish? Ix Bacal? The failure of the *Ch'achac*? As he asked himself these questions, one of Balam's legs began to fall asleep. He wondered if he'd be able to climb from the tree at all when the opportunity came.

Balam knew someone was approaching when he saw the old man look up. Ah Chan's weathered face tightened and his mouth hardened. Cuc and several bachelors, Tutz among them, walked up.

"We have been talking among ourselves," Cuc said before Ah Chan had a chance to greet them. "We would like to ask your advice on an important matter."

Ah Chan nodded, ignoring their rudeness. "I know why you have come." Slowly he stood, towering above them. "We must not create enemies where we do not have enemies." It was as if he knew his great height would lend strength to his words.

Cuc was not daunted. "To not retaliate will be a message to our neighbors that we lack the will to defend ourselves and what is ours." Cuc spoke loudly, as if Ah Chan, from his great height, might not be able to hear well.

"It is true that we must defend what is ours," Ah Chan said. "But we must be cautious. We must strike only when we know for certain from which village the thieves came. Even then we must weigh the benefits of striking. Lives will be lost at a time when we need all the strength we can gather. What if the rains do not come? We must prepare for a difficult future."

Balam watched, not knowing who was right—the bachelors or Ah Chan. In his heart he felt the thumping anger of the bachelors. In his head he knew Ah Chan spoke with wisdom.

"You may be right," said Cuc, the harshness of his voice contradicting his words. "But before we can prepare for the future, we must deal with the present. Now, as we speak, one of our neighbors thinks we are an easy target for kidnapping and theft. Unless we show them otherwise, they will continue to kidnap and steal from us."

"Do you know where Venus lives in the sky? Is this a good time to make war?" Ah Chan paused, knowing the answers to his questions. "We have lived a long time without war," he continued. "We must be careful not to unleash its power. We must put all our energies now into ending the drought . . . into bringing rain. We must not spend our energy waging war against our neighbors."

"We may do both at once," Cuc countered. "We will raid Tzebtun and bring back with us a boy or girl . . . perhaps several . . . for sacrifice. In that way we will send a message to our neighbors that we will not tolerate what has happened to us. At the same time, we will feed the gods the *ch'ulel* of human hearts!"

Balam found Cuc persuasive. Ah Chan's silence made him think that perhaps the old man finally agreed with the bachelors. Instead, Ah Chan shook his head.

"You will only bring upon this village the wrath of our neighbors. You came for my advice. I say that now some things must be suffered."

"Why?" Balam did not see from which bachelor this question came.

"We are not more powerful than the gods and we cannot change those things that are destined to happen. If you do not know these truths, you are young and foolish." Ah Chan snorted. Turning, he stooped, walking into the darkness of his *palapa*.

Balam heard several bachelors mutter as they walked

away. One of them was Tutz. "He is old and tired."

"Yes, and stubborn," said Cantul.

Did Ah Chan think there was nothing to be done? Did he think there was no hope? The more he thought about it, the more Balam could not accept what Ah Chan had said.

When the plaza was empty, Balam climbed down the tree. It felt good to stretch his legs as he ran toward his *palapa*. Balam wanted to speak with his father, to ask his father to reason with Ah Chan, to help Ah Chan see the sense in what the bachelors said.

His father was in the courtyard, sitting by the *palapa* door. Uk held a hand to his mouth. "Nakin is resting. We must be quiet," he said. Balam nodded. Since the maize seed had been stolen, no words would comfort Nakin. She was more certain than ever that this was a bad time in which to bring a child into the world. Her worst fears were becoming true and she felt partly to blame for having given voice to those fears, making them more real.

Balam squatted close, his knee touching his father's knee. He quietly told his father what he'd heard, hoping his father would not ask how he'd been able to hear such talk.

"Ah Chan is right."

Balam could not hide his disappointment. "You think we should do nothing?" He struggled to keep his voice low.

"No. But I think we must wait to do something," Uk said. "Ah Chan is right to be cautious."

"What will we do?" Balam did not like the whining in his own voice, but could not stop it. "We do not have seed."

His father's stare made him uncomfortable, but Balam refused to look away. "That is not true," Uk finally said, his voice as steady as his gaze. "When life is difficult, we must all sacrifice. It will not feed us well, but there are the seeds for your blood crop and your brother's blood crop."

Balam was stunned. He wanted to help his family and village, but planting the seeds of his blood crop seemed desperate.

"To plant one's blood crop, one must be a man," Balam finally said.

"Sometimes we cannot choose the time for manhood. Besides, it is almost time for you to be a man," said Uk.

"To live with the bachelors?"

Finally, Uk looked down. "If you wish, we will discuss this with Ah Chan."

H H H

Balam held tightly to the chopping stick, unable to hide the fury in his face. What would his father think when he came back from the bachelor *palapa,* cast out before he could enter?

"You will be a fine bachelor someday," said Cuc. "But you may not come with us. Indeed you have hunted with us. But we caught nothing . . . we fought no one . . . except Cantul." The bachelors chuckled. "You are still untested and we cannot rely on you in times of need. And," he half smiled, "we do not want to be distracted . . . worrying about your safety and how you might jeopardize our safety."

Balam looked to Tutz, appealing to him with his eyes. Tutz's face was expressionless. Did he agree with what Cuc was saying? Or was he afraid to disagree?

Furious, he glared at the bachelors, one by one. They were freshly painted black, armed with spears and chopping sticks and clubs. They appeared to be shadows, pieces of the night in human form. They were prepared to steal into every nook and corner of Tzebtun like the darkness of night itself, bringing back with them maize seed and also a boy or girl or both for sacrifice.

Helpless, he watched them disappear into the forest, becoming shadows of the shadows in the evening light.

What would his father say?

Swallowing the tears he refused to let slip from his eyes, Balam walked into the forest, careful to keep far enough behind the bachelors so they would not hear him. He was determined to prove he could be trusted in times of need. He was determined to prove he was more man than boy.

As quiet as the bachelors wanted to be, Balam heard their footsteps clearly—too clearly. If he could hear them, the last bachelor in line would be able to hear him. He let them get a little farther ahead, and worked to walk more quietly. But to be more quiet he found himself going more slowly. The footsteps ahead grew faint—too faint. When he could barely hear them, he hurried ahead, heedless of sound.

The shadows of night darkened, growing larger, seeming to swell, fitting together like broken pieces of a soot-covered pot. The moon had not yet risen and the forest canopy blocked from view any stars. As the air cooled, a feeling grew in him that the earth had turned upside down. Is this what it was like for Lord Sun as he walked through Xibalba? He felt as if he were walking inside the nightmare he had had so often.

He had never been so alone in the forest at night, so far from the safety of the village. He struggled to walk quickly enough to keep within the sound of bachelor footsteps, but more than anything now he feared that his own footsteps would be heard by *xtabai* or *zip* or, worse yet, *aluxob*. Were demons roaming the forest, rising from Xibalba, attracted to darkness without moonlight?

A shadow of dread slowly came over Balam. In listening so hard for demons and dwarfs and other forest spirits, he'd lost track of the sound of footsteps ahead. He stopped, silencing his own footsteps, and listened. He heard nothing but the rustling of leaves overhead and the small, sporadic sounds of scurrying in the forest.

He was alone—alone and lost. Where could he be? Without the moon or stars he didn't even know in which direction he faced. Where could the bachelors be? He fought a desire to cry out, to call for them. But that would surely prove to Cuc and all the rest that he was too much a boy to be with them.

Where was he? He stumbled ahead, pawing at the darkness with his free hand, unsure of his footing. With his chopping stick he struck at the darkness, occasionally poking the ground in front of him. He remembered stories of the earth caving in, plunging people into underground rivers that led to *cenotes*—that led to Xibalba. Had the bachelors been swallowed up in this way?

But no. He scolded himself for thinking such a foolish thought. Such a thing would make noise. The bachelors would not have fallen into the earth quietly.

Had the bachelors been discovered by men from another village, Tzebtun perhaps, and captured in the night?

As if in answer to this question, a noise violated the silence to his right. Was it a bachelor, or an enemy? Balam drew closer to a tree that stood between himself and the noise. He heard it again, closer this time. Holding his chopping stick in his mouth, trying not to cut his tongue or the corners of his mouth on the sharp flakes of stone, he scrambled up the tree's trunk. He swung himself up onto the first branch just as he heard a long, low growl.

Quickly scrambling to the next branch, Balam took the stick from his mouth and peered down through the darkness. The jaguar circled the tree, its long tail disappearing only when the nose reappeared. It stopped where Balam had climbed the tree, and looked up.

The eyes were terrifying—yellow, seeming to glow, seeming to illuminate the face that stared at him. Slowly, as if only stretching, it rose up on its hind legs and pawed at the tree trunk, never taking its eyes off Balam. Standing, it looked very much to Balam like his dreamed visions of Lord Sun—human and animal all at once, flexed claws seeming thick as fingers, legs muscled as his father's. Standing, it reached the first branch. The animal bared its teeth and seemed to speak, the sound low and throaty. Its tail twitched and its hind legs tensed to jump.

Balam hit the branch with his stick and the jaguar flinched, made cautious by the sound. Balam took this chance to get a better grip on the stick. If he swung hard and true, the jaguar could not climb the tree without risking injury. How long would he be able to hold the jaguar at bay?

Balam heard a rustling sound in the darkness, growing louder, just beyond the jaguar. Startled, the jaguar turned its head toward the noise. Quickly, seemingly with no effort, it leapt to the first branch.

As Balam grabbed for a higher branch, a low, angry rumble came from the jaguar as it glanced at Balam and then below. The musky smell of peccaries came from the dark before Balam saw them. Following the scent came the herd, big ones and small ones, their legs seeming too small to support their bodies. Balam saw that they were headed toward the tree in which he perched.

Herds of peccaries were dangerous, known to kill anything that got in their way. Balam threw the chopping stick with all his strength, hoping to hit the distracted jaguar, knock it off its branch and into the herd. With a thud, it hit the jaguar in the neck before tumbling to the ground. The peccaries stopped in front of the stick, confused, their bristles rising. Snorting, they looked up.

Balam saw blood, looking black in the night, ooze from the jaguar's wound. In pain the jaguar roared and tried to turn around on the limb, wanting to strike at Balam. With strength he didn't know he had, Balam ripped a branch from the limb on which he stood and hurled that at the jaguar.

The jaguar saw it coming and lurched toward it, swatting with his great paws. And then, to Balam's surprise, it lost its balance. Clawing at the air, it fell to the ground, directly in front of the peccaries.

As fast as the jaguar was, the peccaries were faster. The jaguar leapt to its feet, roaring and swatting. The peccaries swarmed, attacking from all sides, tearing with their tusks. Several peccaries squealed in pain and retreated, only to be replaced by more. Balam prepared to climb higher. What if the jaguar won and came looking for him?

He grabbed a branch, that then came off in his hand. The snarling below grew louder. Dropping the stick, he reached for another branch.

But the noise suddenly stopped and Balam heard

once more the sound of peccaries running away, into the night. He looked down and saw the body of the jaguar, and the bodies of three peccaries. None of them moved. Was it possible the others had been frightened by a stick dropping onto them from the night?

Cautiously, Balam climbed from the tree. He crouched as he approached, first picking up his chopping stick and then creeping toward the jaguar. Its eyes were open, but otherwise it looked dead. Blood still seeped from around its neck and head. More than that, the peccaries had wounded its belly. Guts looped out from the tears.

Could the jaguar truly be dead? Unbelieving, Balam stepped closer, lifting the chopping stick, reaching out to prod the jaguar's body. As he did so, the jaguar reared, its eyes now blazing. Its roar filled Balam's head and he froze, unable to move from claws that raked across his chest.

Falling backward, Balam screamed, clutching his chest. He closed his eyes in pain, expecting the jaguar to pounce, expecting to die. Nothing happened in the silence that followed. Was the jaguar playing with him?

Cautiously, not daring to move any other part of his body, Balam opened his eyes, looking toward his feet. The jaguar had fallen, too.

This time its eyes were closed.

TWELVE

Balam lay stunned for a long time, his eyes closed against the night and the animal lying so close to him. If it were still alive, would it attack?

Cautiously, he turned onto his belly and pushed up onto his hands and knees, facing the animal. The wounds on his chest were beginning to stiffen as the blood hardened. With each breath his skin ached with stretching. Fearful of moving, he watched the jaguar for signs of life. It was too dark to be certain. The jaguar's spots made it difficult to see clearly where the animal ended and darkness began.

Balam found his eyes returning often to stare at the jaguar's head. The fearsome face had changed greatly from the one that had looked up at him as he stood in the tree. Where the open eyes had seemed to glow yellow, illuminating the face, there were only shades of gray and black. Details were difficult to see. He stared anyway, squinting with the effort. The beast no longer appeared angry. Surprisingly, it seemed almost content.

As he stared, the darkness seemed to shift, altering shadows and shapes. He was horrified to see the face slowly grow human-like. What had been contented lines on a jaguar's face did not look content on a human face. Quite the opposite—the more human the jaguar's face appeared, the more furious it grew, until what Balam saw was the face of Lord Sun in his nightmares.

Could it be that he'd killed Lord Sun?

With great effort he tore his gaze from the face, contorted by a jaguar's smile into a human snarl, letting his eyes slide down the jaguar's back, lingering on the still chest before following the line that ended with the tip of its tail. He half expected it to twitch before the jaguar leapt, tired of lying in wait, tired of pretending to be dead.

Balam wanted to scramble to his feet, to turn, to run. He didn't dare. Instead, he slowly lowered himself to the ground, at once fascinated and terrified by the changes he was witnessing.

For how long he sat, Balam did not know. His quiet body grew stiff in the cool night air. As he stared, the terror he felt softened, becoming awe. He sat through the night as if in vigil, respectfully watching the face change back and forth between that of a jaguar and that of an almost-human. He did not grow sleepy even though sitting in the dark, watching the jaguar, was more like dreaming than wakefulness.

The almost-human face was not always the same. Balam was startled, but also reassured, to find the face struggling to look like that of the boy in the *cenote*. Was it his own face or his brother's? Hadn't his brother turned into a jaguar while trying to save Ix Bacal? Balam could only guess whose face it was, using the smile as a clue. He hoped his own smile was less taunting than the one he saw now.

Most startling of all, once during the night he saw what could only be his father's face, contorted in grief. What could be causing his father's face to twist so? Was it something in the past? The future? Or was his father grieving now?

Slowly the face became once more that of a jaguar. Balam knew Lord Sun had escaped Xibalba again—that he, Balam, had not killed Lord Sun—when the face stopped changing altogether, remaining that of a jaguar, growing more distinct as the light grew bolder. The first light through the trees didn't warm. As Lord Sun rose, Balam's shadow fell over the body of the jaguar. His shadow darkened as the light grew stronger, seeming to weigh more heavily on the still body stretched out before him.

With Lord Sun to his back, Balam now knew where he was. The bachelors had indeed been going to Tzebtun, which lay ahead and to his right. His village was in back of him and a little to his left. How far, he did not know. But it couldn't be too far.

Balam stood, stiff as a tree from sitting still so long. A

jabbing pain made him look at his chest. Thin strips of skin hung from the base of the wounds, dried now and slightly curled, dark with blood. It still ached to breathe deeply, to stretch the wounds with their bark of blood.

He took a step toward the jaguar. In the early morning light, the jaguar was magnificent. The tawny color of its fur caught the morning light and held it. The spots were like flakes of the night, disguising blood and dirt. Its paws were huge. The gentle rounded tips of its ears, with tufts of hair feathering out from within, contrasted with the sharp whiteness of its fangs. Its whiskers were long, matching the color of its eyelashes.

The jaguar was undoubtedly dead, but Balam felt fear as he approached it. What power did the jaguar still possess in death that it could transform its face into human faces?

As he stepped closer, and as the light became stronger, Balam was surprised to see worms emerging from the jaguar's coat. Instead of brightening further, the fur seemed to grow dull. Could the jaguar be decomposing as he watched? Balam found himself unable to keep from looking at its terrible wounds, especially those of the belly.

His awe and fear of this animal slowly changed to pity.

What should he do? He could hurry back to the village. But that would mean abandoning the jaguar to the scavengers of the jungle floor. What should he do? The jaguar, even though dead, should be offered to the gods. Its heart should be given to those who could send rain.

The first touch sent a shiver up Balam's arm and down his back. The fur was soft. The leg, all by itself, was heavy, and he found it impossible to lift the body enough to drag it. Perhaps he would have to leave it after all.

From the corner of his eye, he saw the chopping stick. He had helped his father gut and flay deer before, and smaller animals. Always, his father had used a flaying knife, the sharp chipped edge of a stone that fit into the palm of his hand. Balam walked toward the chopping stick and picked it up. The stone chips were sharp. He felt certain it would work, if he were patient.

Balam was prepared for blood, but the jaguar gave up little blood with its skin. The most blood spilled when Balam cut through the neck to separate the head and skin from the rest of the body. Blood also came when he cut paws from the bones and muscle of its legs. Balam was unable to flay the tail, so he simply severed its bones from the hind quarters.

As Lord Sun climbed higher in the sky, the air grew warmer. The carcass became pungent, giving off smells the way it had once given off living heat. Balam was unable to cut through the ribs of the jaguar's chest. Instead he punched a hand under the ribs and up toward the stomach, feeling with his fingers until he grasped the heart, cramped and still. Closing his eyes and gritting his teeth, he twisted and yanked in one movement, as if picking an underripe mango. The heart came out, trailing root-like blood vessels, followed by a blob of congealed blood and parts of lung.

Balam stared. At the end of his blood-slickened arm, in his hand, was the heart of a jaguar. It was not as large as he'd expected—it could have been the heart of a deer. Still, he sensed its power. He would not have been surprised to see it begin beating again in his hand.

From the heart he looked to the carcass. Without its skin or head or paws or tail it could have been the carcass of a large dog or small deer. Already it was attracting flies. An ant crawled over its chest, mingling with the flies. Soon it would attract other scavengers.

Just the pelt and head were almost heavier than he could carry. To help, he rested the base of the jaguar's head on the top of his own and draped the rest of the pelt over his shoulders and back. The skin, sticky on the inside, clung to his own skin, seeming to scab to him as it dried. He shrugged, feeling as if the jaguar's skin had grown onto his own.

Crossing the front legs over his chest, he held the paws together. On the paws he rested the heart. It was as if the jaguar were offering its own heart to the gods.

Pulled up as far as possible around his shoulders, the pelt still dragged on the ground. He started on his way— it was the best he could do. Looking back, he saw the winding trail of the dragged tail, looking similar to the track of a snake.

Walking along, smelling the jaguar's blood and fur and skin, feeling the heaviness of the jaguar's head on his own, he soon forgot the heaviness of his load. Instead, he felt as if he were inside the jaguar, had become the jaguar's bones and muscle. He felt as if he were giving his life to the jaguar just as the jaguar's heart would give life back to the village. At first the skin tugged at his own skin where it had scabbed. But soon Balam's walk became smooth, fitting the skin, and the tugging stopped. It was as if he had become the jaguar—full of power and grace, full of anger and cunning, full of purpose.

Had he become the jaguar, guardian of *milpa*, relative of the rain gods, the embodiment of Lord Sun? He smelled of jaguar. He looked of jaguar. Blood from the jaguar's head slowly dripped onto his forehead, cheeks, and chin. He moved more and more like a jaguar, stalking more than walking, hunched over from the weight of the pelt, the front paws dangling now, swinging as if walking to the rhythm of Balam's movements. Holding the heart in both hands, tight to his own chest, Balam felt as if the jaguar's life had somehow entered his own.

Walking in this way, he found himself noticing things about the forest that he wouldn't ordinarily notice—the flit of a bird from one tree to the next—a smell that told him an opossum was nearby. He walked from shadow to shadow, as quietly as a shadow. He noticed how dead the forest had become, how empty of life. He felt the hunger of the jaguar in his own stomach, its longing for game, for rain. He felt the rage of a jaguar who had been so weak it had suffered worms under its skin while it was alive, a jaguar so weak it had lost its footing in a tree, so weak it could not fight off a pack of peccaries.

Had he become a *uay*? Had he been transformed into a jaguar? Had the jaguar's face he'd seen in the *cenote* been his own? Or perhaps the jaguar had been a *uay*, having transformed itself into Balam the boy, and was just now returning to its true form.

Balam stepped onto the path leading to the village. He was so lost in these thoughts that he didn't notice Ix Bacal's mother walking toward him. He didn't see the terror on her face as she spun around, running as if being chased. He only looked up as he came to the first *palapa*. It surprised him that nobody was about.

Heat from Lord Sun seemed to add to the weight of the jaguar pelt as he trudged toward the plaza and Ah Chan's *palapa*. The slickness of sweat was loosening the jaguar skin's hold on his own. Walking now with his feet dragging he felt human again—more boy than man— weak and clumsy, helpless—as if his own skin no longer fit his own body. It was as if the jaguar had consumed him, swallowed him whole, and he could barely move or breathe inside the jaguar's belly.

Even the heart in his hands seemed to change, becoming smaller and harder, less like the heart of a jaguar and more like a lump of clay left out in the sun.

He stared at it as he came upon the plaza. Looking up, he was surprised to see a silent crowd gathered under the great ceiba tree. All eyes, including his father's, followed him as he walked. Towering above all those gathered was Ah Chan.

Balam not only saw fear in their faces, he could smell it. Even his own father looked as if he were staring not at Balam but at an apparition.

Ah Chan stepped forward and Balam sensed a wariness in the old man he'd never sensed before.

"Balam?"

Balam nodded, his head heavy with the weight of the jaguar's head resting on his own. "Here. I bring you the heart of a jaguar." Balam handed the heart to Ah Chan.

Ah Chan took it, bowing his head slightly. "Will you come sit with me?" He nodded toward his *palapa*.

"Yes." Balam looked toward his father. "Help take the jaguar from my back."

Uk stepped forward and with shaking hands peeled the skin from his son's shoulders. The skin pulled, hurting in places, seeming almost to tear his own skin—as if he himself were being flayed. Balam reached up to lift the head. It slipped from his hands, dropping heavily onto the back of his head. Balam felt one of the large teeth scrape downward just as he turned to catch the jaguar's head better.

He found himself staring directly into the jaguar's face, his nose almost touching its nose. Stepping back, he saw that from its mouth dangled a lock of his hair, torn from his scalp. Up against the teeth was caught the white bead Balam had worn to signify he was a boy.

Ah Chan stepped forward. "In more ways than one, this jaguar has made you a man," he said. "Come."

Balam felt Ah Chan's hand on his shoulder and let himself be led to the old man's *palapa*. He sat, too exhausted to squat, and watched several men, including his father, gather around the jaguar, now spread out on the floor.

"Tell us how you came upon this jaguar," said Ah Chan, quietly.

Balam told them of following the bachelors, of losing them, of hearing sounds, of climbing the tree, of the jaguar and the peccaries, of the kill. He told them of his vigil and his visions, and of flaying the jaguar. He described how he felt, wrapped in the skin of a jaguar, the head of a jaguar resting on his own head.

When he finished, no one spoke for a long time.

Finally, Ah Chan broke the silence. "We have news of the bachelors. A messenger from Tzebtun came not long ago to say that all of them have been captured. At the end of three days they will be sacrificed, one by one, unless we can offer up the best from among us to the gods." He lifted his head, as if beseeching the gods to listen. "And they are right. For too long we have not given up one of our own. For too long we have not given of our best. It is time."

Again there was silence.

"Before you arrived, we were discussing who among us was the best." Ah Chan stared at Balam, his eyes steady. "Now we know who it is we must sacrifice."

Balam looked from Ah Chan to his father. His father was silent, struggling to subdue the grief on his face. Tears fell from his eyes as he looked at his son. It was the face of his father he'd seen last night in the face of the jaguar.

Balam looked to the jaguar, spread out before him, the bead of his youth still tangled in its teeth. It had not found death pleasing to face. But it had faced death bravely.

He looked up to Ah Chan and then to his father. There were no words adequate enough to say he knew too.

Part IV

Blue from the North

The hardest part of preparing wasn't the fasting—lately his stomach had been empty more than it had been full. The hardest part wasn't being under Ah Chan's constant care and guidance. The hardest part of preparing for sacrifice was being by himself, especially at night.

When he was by himself at night, in a small *palapa* that had been hastily built next to Ah Chan's, his mind filled with thoughts and images that were startling and strange, many of them frightening. The darkness inside the *palapa* seemed to become the darkness inside his head. The ceiling became the inside of his skull. The single door became his eyes and nose and mouth, all in one.

To feel that his head had grown to the size of the *palapa* was unbearable—his feelings and his thoughts would crowd too close to see properly, would grow too large to understand. And then he would panic—his breath becoming quick and shallow, sweat dripping from his face and chest, his heart beating faster and faster. The only thing that stopped his panic was to step into the night air. Outside, he could breathe again and his head returned to its rightful size. Outside, his thoughts and feelings stepped back a respectful distance. Outside, he returned to being himself.

Tonight, when he could bear it no longer, he walked out into the night air, breathing deeply, closing his eyes and throwing back his head. Ah Chan had spent the day instructing him, telling him of the things he might expect to encounter in the Underworld—who he would meet—who was dangerous or good, powerful or weak. The old man had talked of so many things, Balam's head felt crowded as a beehive, buzzing with things to remember, single things lost in the sound of many things combined.

From the droning only one thing stood out: "Be prepared to retrace the steps of your life. As you travel the White *Sacbe* you may relive parts of your life in ways you don't now remember."

Balam opened his eyes and found himself gazing into a night sky without moon or clouds, strewn with stars that seemed remarkably close. The band of stars, the White *Sacbe*, arced across the sky. Never before had he seen it so clearly. It looked like a road paved with crushed limestone so white it could have been crushed pieces of the moon.

The immensity of the sky overwhelmed him. It began to move, looking like the ruffled water of the *cenote*, with stars on top instead of floating leaves, moving farther apart and then closer together, floating and sinking and rising once more to the water's surface. The shimmering movement of the sky made him feel faint, off balance, about to fall. He reached out to catch himself and, to his astonishment, he seemed to fall upward instead of down. Up, up he fell—into the sky, toward the White *Sacbe* itself.

ℍ   ℍ   ℍ

Although the walking was effortless, the brightness of the road hurt his eyes, making it impossible to see where he was going. Slowly, as his eyes became used to the light, he saw the White *Sacbe* stretching ahead, glowing. On either side were trees hung with lianas and filled with birds. Paths branched off the road he was traveling, some of them wide and well-used.

The sound of his footsteps seemed to echo, as if he were walking in a cave—or as if someone were following him. He turned and peered behind. The *sacbe* was empty.

As he turned back and continued to walk, he heard the sound of people approaching from all around him. Suddenly, people began swarming from the many forest paths, joining each other on the White *Sacbe*, all of them going in Balam's direction. All of these people were talking excitedly, sounding more like macaws than people, greeting each other, sharing gossip and *balche*. He was soon caught up in a huge, moving crowd of people, feeling as if he were caught up in a celebration—of what, Balam was uncertain.

Balam didn't know when the crowd must have left the *sacbe*. He noticed only when he found himself entering a great playing field, flanked on either side by huge stone steps onto which the crowd of people swarmed. He climbed the stone steps and stood near the top, looking down at the flatness of the playing field's trampled dirt.

The crowd grew silent as two groups of men came onto the field. One group was dressed in long, flowing yellow *ex*, the other group in blue *ex*. The men of both groups wore their hair pulled up, reminding Balam of maize tassels, feathers sticking out where their hair was gathered. As they ran, shoulder yokes flapped upon their chests. Their hips and forearms were large with padding.

The men stood facing a columned platform at the head of the field. To the edge of this platform stepped a great lord, draped in jaguar pelts, his hair festooned in the largest and brightest feathers Balam had ever seen, his *ex* of many colors hanging almost to his feet in front. In his hands he held what looked like a large ball.

Holding the ball out over the edge of the platform the lord spoke, almost softly. Even so, his voice carried to every part of the field and to the crowd—as if he were speaking from everywhere at once. "May your game please the gods." He dropped the ball and the men below converged to keep it from touching the ground.

One of the men slid under it, sending the ball spinning upwards with his hip. Down the ball came, bellowing, and Balam saw that it was not a ball at all, but a severed, living head—the head of Lord Sun!

The crowd sprang to life, shouting and screaming, as the players below kept Lord Sun's head in play—bouncing it off chests and thighs, aiming it upward with hips. The men ran with remarkable speed, the head going back and forth among them. The head cursed the players wearing blue and shouted directions to those in yellow. The head moved fast, sometimes changing directions in midair with its nodding or shaking. And then the head began to bite at the men wearing blue, tearing off chunks of padding or flesh. It startled them with roars, like those of a jaguar.

The injured men began to stagger and those wearing yellow danced as they ran, singing praises to themselves and to Lord Sun. The crowd jeered and the men in yellow taunted as they took control of the head. With increasing confidence, they sent it often toward a ring of rock set high alongside the field, just below the steps from which the crowd now threw pebbles and calabashes, empty now of *balche*.

Finally, soaring and cheering as it went, the head flew through the stone ring and rolled back to the middle of the field. The crowd was stunned to silence. The only sound that could be heard was the head laughing, rolling back and forth with the force of its own continuous laughter, never seeming to need to draw a breath.

The great lord came forward. "Silence!" he commanded, and the force of his voice made his anger echo back and forth across the playing field. Lord Sun's head stopped laughing, rolling upright to face the great lord. When at last the echoing stopped, the great lord spoke again.

"Lord Sun's team has won today, as we all have seen. But I fear Lord Sun has grown too strong. Therefore, it will not be the losers who forfeit their heads today, but the winners. Let us sacrifice the best team we have seen this day, not the second best!"

Balam was startled by the cheering that followed, coming from the crowd. Above the cheering could be heard the voice of Lord Sun, shouting in anger, spinning around and around, faster and faster.

Balam watched in horror as, one by one, the men dressed in yellow knelt and their heads were chopped off. Blood spewed from their necks, sparkling with *ch'ulel*. The packed dirt glistened with their blood.

Lord Sun's shouting grew louder with each man's severed head until the stones of the steps began to shake and clatter. Panic seized Balam and he began weaving his way through the crowd, making his way down the steps, toward the place he had entered the playing field. Lord Sun's shouting grew louder still and rocks began to crumble. Startled, Balam saw the playing field split apart. The earth became a mouth, swallowing Lord Sun's head and the men of both teams as tongues of fire licked its lips. Deep laughter bubbled from the mouth as the split in the earth curved. From where Balam stood it formed what looked like a painful smile—from where the Great Lord stood, waving his arms in anger, it must have looked like a frown. From this smile emerged Lord Sun, a giant now, holding his own head. As if crowning himself, Lord Sun set his head upon his shoulders.

A fearful silence filled the air. Balam felt for a moment as if he'd been struck deaf. Lord Sun slowly turned, his eyes menacing as they scanned the nervous crowd. "Balam!" he cried. "Balam!" To his horror, Balam found himself looking directly into those eyes that glowed with a mixture of hatred and anger and pride.

The crowd stirred around him, uncomfortable as Balam. "Who is this Balam?" he heard a nearby man mutter. Balam crouched, wanting to shrink into the stones.

"Here I am, the one you seek!" came a cry from the other end of the steps. Balam looked up in surprise to see his twin standing above the crowd, having jumped onto the back of a man and climbed onto the man's shoulders. He straddled the man's head, holding a fistful of hair for balance, his other arm held high.

Lord Sun's gaze shifted and the crowd began to murmur Balam's name in a way that sounded dangerous.

Balam caught his breath as his twin leapt from the man's shoulders, agile as a monkey, and disappeared into the crowd. Lord Sun roared, bloody spittle spraying from his mouth. Crouching low, Balam stumbled down the steps, groping between legs, feeling pushed from behind as the crowd began to panic and flee. He feared being trampled now as he neared the bottom stair. Just as he jumped to the ground, he felt a tugging at his elbow. Turning, he saw his twin brother.

"How . . ." he began to ask. His brother jerked hard, silencing him, and steered him into the forest, away from the masses of people surging off the stairs.

"I ran between many legs, tangling them as I went," his twin replied, smiling. "I am good at going unseen. I have followed you, unseen, every day of your life . . . watching and waiting, waiting for this day. Come!" his brother ordered. "This way!"

They ran through the forest, following no trail, until the shouts and cries from the field were faint, no more than the whisper of wind through the leaves. When they stepped from the forest, Balam's eyes were once more blinded by the light shining from the White *Sacbe*.

"I have brought him," Balam heard his brother say, letting go of his arm.

Balam peered about as his eyes gradually became used to the light. Dimly, as if through fog, he saw his mother and Ix Bacal standing before him.

"I have waited a long time for you to join me," his mother said. "Let us retrace the steps of your life together . . . the four of us. In seeing your life not only through your own eyes, but also through ours, your journey will be more complete."

H H H

Balam felt the cold hardness of the ground on his back. His head was sore where he'd fallen on it. Even before he opened his eyes, the familiar voice of Ah Chan broke into his consciousness.

"You are weak from fasting," the old man said, helping Balam to his feet. "Let me help you inside."

Once inside the *palapa*, Ah Chan listened to his blood, taking his pulse at his elbow, wrist, and neck. As the old man listened, his eyebrows slowly raised. "You have been traveling," he finally said, his voice low, respectful.

Balam nodded. "And I have much farther to go." Balam smiled. "But I will not be alone."

THIRTEEN

Balam breathed in deeply the smell of copal, and watched one of the village elders sprinkle more of the resin onto the small fire inside his *palapa*. By the light falling in through the door, Balam could tell Lord Sun was almost at his zenith. It was almost time for this day to end and a new day to begin, for Balam to leave this life to begin his journey in the next life.

That morning Balam had awakened, feeling refreshed, having slept well and long for the first time since he'd been fasting, preparing.

"Good morning," Ah Chan had said, shaking Balam's arm. And then Ah Chan handed Balam several tortillas. There was something odd about their smell, until Balam realized they were made of maize.

"These will strengthen your blood . . . give it *itz* . . . make it more nourishing to the gods," Ah Chan had told him.

Before, when he tried, Balam had been unable to

remember the taste of maize. His first bite of these tortillas brought to life more than the taste of maize. It brought back the firm, fleshy feel of maize to his mouth—the smell of maize to his nose—the reassuring comfort of maize resting in his stomach. With that first bite, Balam knew more surely than ever that the gods had made humans of maize. He could feel the power of maize spreading outward to every part of his body, making him quiver like the leaves of a maize plant in a breeze.

Balam had felt calm all morning, calm enough to sense a nervousness in Ah Chan and the four elders. They had seemed unusually careful about what they had said this morning, how they had acted, as if they expected Balam to panic or to suddenly realize what was about to happen.

But Balam knew what was to happen. For seven days and nights he'd been preparing for it. He knew and, especially after the dream he'd had several nights ago, he was not afraid.

There had been times, though, when he'd been sad. Yesterday he'd been allowed to say good-bye to his family. What had made it sad was not being able to touch anybody. That had been hard—standing several arm-lengths from them and being able to use only words to express his love for them, to say good-bye.

He'd hidden some of his sadness in joking.

"You were more upset about the dog than about me," he'd said to Tooch, trying not to smile.

His brother's eyes had widened in horror. "No, that is not true," he'd begun, until he saw the laughter in Balam's eyes. Tooch had looked at his feet, embarrassed.

Balam fought an urge to hug his brother, to reassure him. Instead, he said, "Brother, I would like you to have the seeds for my blood crop. Plant them, and may they help you and your family prosper. My chopping stick is yours also."

He had turned to his *chichi* and said, "Soon you will have maize to grind instead of breadnuts."

His *chichi's* mouth had stretched into a grimace. Was she about to cry or smile? She'd reached out to him, realized what she was doing, and dropped her arms to her sides. "We will be together in the afterlife," she'd said, "sooner than later."

Uk's face had been unusually stony. "I am proud of you," he'd said.

"You have taught me well," Balam had replied, able to see now the feelings his father was hiding, had always tried to hide.

It was hardest, by far, to say good-bye to Nakin. She had been such a good mother to him and it seemed almost like a betrayal of her to look forward, as he did, to being with X'tactani. "You did not give me life," he said, "but you gave me love. I will always be your son."

Nakin had managed to smile. "I remember when you were born," she said. "You were so small, so weak. But I was certain then that, being small, you would grow more and work harder and become greater than many others. I was right." She had looked at Balam with a clarity he hadn't seen in her face for a long time.

His memories and thoughts were interrupted by itching. Blue paint now covered his entire body. In drying it cracked, seeming to crack his skin also. He dared not scratch, fearful of peeling off the paint that was the sacred color of the Chacs. Before painting him, Ah Chan and the elders had bathed him carefully, spreading the juice of the aloe onto him, rubbing it in before covering him in blue.

Ah Chan stood at the door. "Come," he said. Balam stood and walked outside. The brightness of the day made him feel that he might be walking into a fire instead of the plaza. Around the *palapa* he and Ah Chan went. He knew what was expected. He had fasted, drinking only virgin water, for seven days. Under the old man's supervision he urinated one last time. He did not want to foul himself on the altar.

"Would you like a calming drink?" Ah Chan asked, when Balam was through.

"No," he said. He felt calm enough. Over time he felt he'd already let go of this life. He was ready, not wanting to linger more, to wait more, to say good-bye more. More than ever, he felt between—between this world and that, night and dawn, boyhood and manhood, life and death.

⋈   ⋈   ⋈

The village had gathered under the ceiba tree. They watched, silent, as Balam emerged from the *palapa*. Balam looked over each face. In some he saw pity. In some he saw admiration. In some he saw nothing but curiosity.

As he followed Ah Chan toward the altar built of cut stones from the ruins, he searched the horizon one last time for clouds. There were none. But that would change. Surely his heart, his *ch'ulel*, his life, would bring *hahah*.

Ah Chan raised his voice, crying to the Chacs. "To you we give the best we have. We give gladly, knowing you will send us rain, alive with *itz*. We send you our plea with this worthy boy."

Of everything to become used to, this was the hardest: He would never become a man—he would always remain a boy. But, Ah Chan had told him, boys could go where men would be noticed. Boys could carry messages as well as men, perhaps better.

As Ah Chan continued, Balam noticed with surprise the bachelors, huddled together. They had been freed? And then he noticed, behind them, a group of strange, grim-faced men. Balam almost smiled, realizing these strangers were men from Tzebtun, come to watch the sacrifice before releasing the bachelors, who were now their captives. Each bachelor face was as hardened as a clay figure—each face except Tutz's. His eyes appeared puffed and his chin trembled. Balam wanted to speak to Tutz, to tell him that he would give the bachelor's greetings to his sister in the Underworld. Balam wanted to speak, but Ah Chan was finished speaking. The silence could not be broken.

Balam stepped up to the altar, and then turned his back to it, to Tutz. He faced the red of east, from where the rains came, from where Lord Sun was born each day. The four elders helped him lie back on the altar. The smooth stones were warm, soothing.

Each elder held a leg or an arm. They were gentle but firm, pulling his legs apart, holding his arms high. Balam's limbs pointed in the four directions. He felt for a moment as if he had become the four directions—as if he could reach from horizon to horizon. His chest seemed to grow with each breath, as if it were becoming the center of the world—the place where the sacred ceiba would erupt.

Ah Chan approached from the side. He had counseled Balam to close his eyes when this moment came. Now, looking at Ah Chan from the corners of his eyes, Balam suspected Ah Chan wished his, Balam's, eyes closed as much for the comfort of himself as for Balam.

Towering over him, looking down, Ah Chan's face was in shadow. It was a face at once familiar and strange. Only the old man's eyes were alive—and fierce, as if Ah Chan had transformed himself into a jaguar.

Ah Chan raised his hand. In it was clasped the flint

knife, the Hand of God, which flashed like lightning in the sun. Balam closed his eyes against its flashing, but fear came over him in the darkness of his head.

As he opened his eyes, the knife came down.

The force of the knife pushed out all his air. His legs and arms became rigid and his eyes widened, his mouth gaped. Balam did not feel pain as much as he was surprised to see his own heart, beating in Ah Chan's hand.

And then, his eyes still open, darkness fell as blood rained down upon his face.

GLOSSARY

Maya words should be pronounced phonetically. The vowels are:

a as in "father"

e as in "prey"

i sounded as a double *e*, as in "see"

o as in "hello"

u sounded as a double *o*, as in "zoo"—except, when followed by any other vowel, it sounds like a *w*

As for consonants, *x* is pronounced with the *sh* sound and *c* is pronounced like a *k*. The *j* is pronounced like an *h*. Glottalized consonants (not used in English) are pronounced with the voice box closed and are signaled with an apostrophe following the letter. In other words, the tongue forms the sound but the speaker appears to swallow the sound. Only the force of breath in the mouth causes the letter's sound to be heard.

The accents of Maya words are almost always on the last syllable.

ahman — [ah mahn'] a priest or shaman. There were many levels of priests, and some specialization. In most villages he was a jack-of-all-trades, a combination of medical doctor and spiritual leader (the spirit and the body were not separate in Maya thinking).

aluxob — [ah loosh ob'] a strong forest elf.

Bacabob — [baa kah bob'] four bearded giant gods who hold up the sky at its four sides.

balche — [ball chae'] an alcoholic drink made from combining water, honey, and the bitter bark of the balché tree. Used for ceremonies and celebrations because it was thought to purify one of evil.

Ben — [ben] the day of Ben, the Reed, one of twenty names given the days of each month. Each name was also matched with a number, running consecutively one through thirteen, some numbers being more powerful and luckier than others, thereby strengthening or weakening the luck of each day's name.

blood crop — a man's first crop of maize, using seeds onto which blood from his umbilical cord was shed after he was born.

calabash — [cal' a bash] a dried and hollowed gourd used for carrying water or storing food.

ceiba — [see baa'] the silk-cotton tree, sacred for the Maya, said to stand in the exact center of the earth. Its roots penetrate Xibalba and its branches reach out to the heavens.

cenote — [sen o' te] a sinkhole deep enough to fill with water from underground rivers. Used for drawing drinking water. Because *cenotes* were also considered openings to Xibalba, offerings (objects as well as animals and humans) were sometimes thrown into them.

Ch'achac — [ch ach aak'] a three-day ceremony, appealing to the Chacs for rain.

Chichén Itzá — [chee chen' eet za'] one of the greatest of Maya cities, located in the heart of the Yucatán, and flourishing from A.D. 400 to A.D. 1200.

chichi — [chee chee'] grandmother.

ch'ulel — [ch oo lil'] bloody holiness, the common soul of men and gods, found in blood.

copal — [koe pall'] incense made from the dried resin of the copal tree.

ex — [esh] the loincloth worn by bachelors and men, made of a strip of woven cotton or beaten bark.

hahah — [ha ha'] the rainy season, necessary for germination of planted maize.

holche — [hole chae'] the chopping down of undergrowth in a *milpa* in preparation for planting maize. The chopped undergrowth is allowed to dry and is then burned.

huipil — [hee peel'] smock-like dress worn by women, made of cotton or pounded bark and sometimes embroidered around the neck in designs that symbolize the universe, its four directions, various gods or planets. It is not a coincidence that the head emerges through the center of these designs.

itz — [eats] blessed substance, the stuff of life, found in the secretions of living things (tears, semen, milk, sap, and nectar, for example). The *itz* of the Chacs is found in rain, where it makes its way to plant and animal life.

Itzamná — [eet zam na'] the most powerful lord of the heavens, the creator god. Translated, his name means "lizard house."

Ix — [ish] the day of Ix, that of the Jaguar. (For more information on day names see Ben.)

Ix Chel — [ish chel] the goddess of the moon, the wife of Lord Sun, the mistress of Venus. To women, she was the goddess of fertility and childbirth.

Kankin — [can keen'] the month of the Yellow Sun, the fourteenth of eighteen twenty-day months of the year (a nineteenth, and unlucky month, had five days).

kinkajou — [keen ka jew'] a monkey-like forest spirit, therefore mischievous.

metate — [meh ta' teh] the partially hollowed stone on which maize or other foods were ground into paste or powder.

milpa — [meel' pa] a field where maize is cultivated. Often squashes and peppers are grown among the maize.

opps — [oohps] the flat stone, laid across three hearth stones, for cooking (especially tortillas).

palapa — [pa la' pa] dwellings made of upright poles and covered with thatch. Perfectly suited for the climate, they protected the Maya from rain and also were cool.

sacbe — [sak bay'] road, often perfectly straight and paved with crushed limestone. The White or Great *Sacbe* refers to the Milky Way. Great *sacbes* often connected cities, or in the case of Chichén Itzá, the city center with its sacred *cenote*.

uay — [woo aye'] people who are able to turn themselves into animal forms.

wac — [waak] a mild form of profanity.

Xibalba — [she ball ba'] the Underworld, inhabited by nine Lords of Night. Akin to the European vision of Hell.

xtabai — [sh ta buy'] a spirit inhabiting ceiba trees, taking the form of a beautiful, but deadly, woman who preys on unsuspecting men.

yax — [yash] a color, dark blue-green, resembling jade or forest leaves.

yum kaax — [yoom kash] forest spirits, usually not friendly to humans.

zip — [zeep] protective forest spirits able to transform themselves into small deer, thereby luring hunters from real deer.

zuhuy ha — [zoo hooy' ha] virgin water, never touched by humans, usually gathered in sacred caves or in standing pools after rain.

SELECTED AND ANNOTATED
BIBLIOGRAPHY

In addition to spending time in the Yucatán, I used over four dozen books to research this novel. I recommend the following as a start for those readers interested in discovering more about the Maya.

FICTION

Rain Player, David Wisniewski (Clarion, 1991) is a wonderful picture book for helping visualize Maya people, architecture, clothing, and natural settings. The story is also great fun.

The Corn Grows Ripe, Dorothy Rhoads (Viking, 1956) is a short, quiet novel that draws the reader immediately into the Maya world of the twentieth century. Set in the Yucatán, it makes me realize how much of the ancient Maya culture has survived to the present day.

The Bright Feather, Dorothy Rhoads (Doubleday, 1932) is a collection of modern Maya folktales. Delightful. It should be noted that Dorothy Rhoads' sister was married to one of the greatest of all Maya scholars, Sylvanus Morley.

Maya Folktales, James Sexton (Anchor, 1992) is a collection of folklore from Guatemala. Although the Maya of Guatemala differ in some respects from the Maya of the lowlands in the Yucatán, there are many common threads and traditions—one being a sense of playfulness and fun.

The Bird Who Cleans the World, Victor Montejo (Curbstone Press, 1991) is a collection of fables that show how animals fit into the Maya view of the universe.

NONFICTION

The Mystery of the Ancient Maya, Carolyn Meyer and Charles Gallenkamp (McElderry, 1995) is a great introduction to this culture, told with authority and style.

Maya, Charles Gallenkamp (Penguin, 1987) is a more detailed introduction to the Maya and the Mayanists who brought this civilization to light. I don't know of a more accessible overview of the Maya for a general audience.

Lost Kingdoms of the Maya, Gene and George Stuart (National Geographic Society, 1993) is full of great photos, but please read the text. It is conversational and covers a wide range of topics concerning the Maya, ancient and modern. Also look in your library for the Stuarts' *The Mysterious Maya,* published also by the National Geographic Society in 1977 and no longer in print.

The Rise and Fall of Maya Civilization, Eric Thompson (University of Oklahoma Press, 1966) is fact-filled but also contains some lovely fictional vignettes that allow the reader to see the Maya as real people, not just anthropological subjects. By one of the great Maya scholars.

The Ancient Maya, Sylvanus Morely, George Brainerd, and Robert Sharer (Stanford University Press, 1983) is the heavily revised classic, originally written in 1946 by the great Mayanist, Morely. Sometimes heavy going, but skip through it often—something will grab you each time.

Maya Cosmos, David Freidel, Linda Schele, and Joy Parker (Morrow, 1993) is a fact-filled, yet at times highly personal, accounting of the latest breakthroughs in what we know about the Maya. It gets pretty technical at times, but is also extremely moving. Searching for the ancient Maya has obviously changed the lives of Freidel and Schele in profound ways.

Look also for *A Forest of Kings*, by Schele and Freidel, and *The Blood of Kings*, by Schele and Mary Ellen Miller (Miller also wrote, with Karl Taube, *The Gods and Symbols of Ancient Mexico and the Maya*, a fascinating illustrated dictionary).

For those of you who want even more, look for John Stephens' *Incidents of Travel in Yucatan*, Vols. I and II (Dover, 1963) which describe this gentleman's adventures in 1841 with his artist friend Frederick Catherwood (Catherwood's classic etchings fill these books). Friar Diego de Landa's *Yucatan* (Dover, 1978) is a translation of a book written in 1566, one of the most important concerning the Maya, ironically by a man who burned all the Maya books he could find, thereby robbing posterity of much of the greatness of Maya learning and literature. And last, but not least, *The Popol Vuh* is the Mayan book of creation (which includes the story of the Hero Twins) and comes in many editions. I recommend the translation by Dennis Tedlock (Simon & Schuster, 1985) or, for those who want a shortened version, *The Essence of Popol Vuh*, by Charles Barnett (Exceptional Books, 1989).